Ramsey Sound
By RR Gordon

Ramsey Sound, Book 2 of the Wish You Were Here series.
Issue 04

Copyright © 2024 by RR Gordon

Cover photograph is the copyright of Nadia Isakova.
To see the full range of Nadia's stunning photography please visit www.photosbest.com
To buy framed prints please visit www.allposters.co.uk and search for "Isakova".

The places in this story are real, but the characters are fictional.

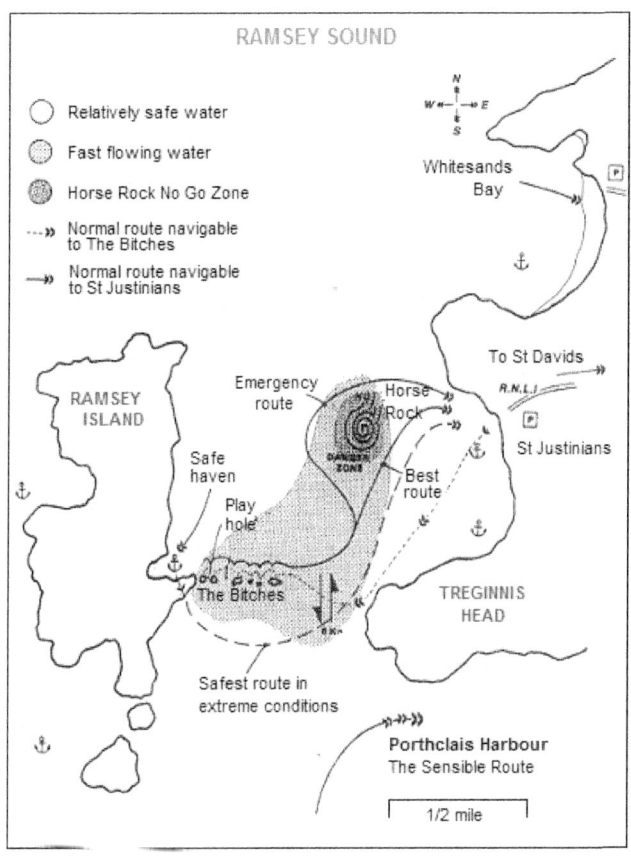

RAMSEY SOUND

N
W ← + → E
S

○ Relatively safe water

◉ Fast flowing water

◉ Horse Rock No Go Zone

···» Normal route navigable to The Bitches

—» Normal route navigable to St Justinians

Whitesands Bay

RAMSEY ISLAND

Emergency route

Horse Rock

To St Davids

R.N.L.I.

St Justinians

Safe haven

DANGER ZONE

Best route

Play hole

The Bitches

B.R.

TREGINNIS HEAD

Safest route in extreme conditions

Porthclais Harbour
The Sensible Route

1/2 mile

CONTENTS

1. Personal Call. Saundersfoot. End of March.

"Good morning, Huntly & Meldrum. How may I help you?"

"Could I speak to Sophie Atkinson please?"

"Who may I say is calling?"

"Dan."

"Dan ….?"

"Yes. Dan."

"May I take your surname please?"

"It's just a personal call."

"Nevertheless, it is our policy to take surnames. Sorry."

"Dan … er … Kernow."

"From …?"

"From nowhere in particular."

"Is there a company name?"

"No."

"May I say the reason for your call?"

Dan sighed. "As I said a second ago, it's just a personal call."

The receptionist paused for a second. "That's fine. Let me see if she's available."

Dan wondered if the security was as strict at Buckingham Palace. The phone system started playing Mendelssohn's Violin Concerto in E Minor

The receptionist came back on the line. "I'm sorry she's in a meeting. May I take a message?"

"No thanks. I'll give her another try tomorrow. Is there a good time to call tomorrow? Do you know if she's in any meetings?"

"I'm afraid I don't know."

"Okay thanks anyway," Dan said, sighing once again.

2. Whiplash & Other Injuries. London. End of March.

"Hi Richard. How are you?" said Andrew Muir.

"Fine thanks, Andrew. Grab a seat." Richard Atkins was Andrew's boss.

They were in Richard's office at the firm's headquarters in Chancery Lane on the edge of the City of London. Formerly detective inspectors in the police force, Richard and his business partner had started a small firm called DHC to perform investigative work for a firm of lawyers. They had rented a small room in their client's premises and soon afterwards they had employed a young Andrew Muir directly from university.

After a few years the business grew out of the little space on the fourth floor of their clients' building and DHC bought their own office a few doors along the road. A decade later Richard's company worked for many other law firms along with a variety of financial organisations that traded in the square mile of the City.

Andrew sat down opposite his boss. "How was your skiing holiday, Richard?"

"Oh it was great, thanks. The apartment was right at the bottom of one of the main runs into Whistler village and you could ski practically to the back door. And the powder was amazing."

Andrew snorted. "I know you can't have skied off-piste, Richard – it was only your second week skiing."

"You're right," laughed Richard. "I spent most of the day in the bar at the top of the slopes, then a few more drinks in the jacuzzi back in the hotel. But somebody in the hotel said that it was the best powder they'd seen for years. All looks the same to me."

Andrew shook his head. He liked his employer, but as the main salesman for the business, Richard Atkins was sometimes a bit loose with the facts for his liking. At the same time Andrew realised that it was Richard's business ideas that had made DHC the size it was today.

"Anyway," Richard continued, "what's been happening while I've been away? Anything new with Cullen?"

The ZBS Banking Group had engaged DHC to trace Stephen Cullen, a former employee who had stolen a large sum of money from the bank.

Richard had assigned Andrew Muir to lead the team hunting for Cullen, but the case had been dormant for nearly nine months. Cullen had nearly been caught the previous summer, working under the assumed name of Dan Lawrie in a pub in north Cornwall, but had evaded capture at the last moment. Since that day there had been no trace of him.

"I'm afraid not. We still haven't got anything back from Iceland."

"Really? It's been three months. You said it would be sorted by the time I got back."

"What I said was: you'll be lucky if it's sorted by the time you get back. Anyway, I can tell you now that Iceland won't be the end of the money trail. Don't forget Cullen was a banking expert. Several times we thought that we'd worked it out, but it just gets more complicated."

"So the money went from ZBS to Switzerland to the Caymans –
"

"No, from Switzerland to Dublin then the Caymans. Then about three places in Africa where he knew the records would be poor, then Iceland just before the whole thing came tumbling down."

"Perhaps he lost it?"

"Perhaps, but I doubt it. He must have known the house of cards was going to collapse leading to mass confusion. He probably sent the money there and then out again the same day, but now nobody knows what happened during that period. And the Icelandic government don't want to admit that they don't have a clue so I think they're just stalling."

"Can't ZBS put any pressure on them like they did with Switzerland?"

"We only got Switzerland sorted because the ZBS parent company is over there. Anyway let's just leave it with Nigel. He's the accountant. If he can't work it out then nobody can."

"Yes," said Richard. "He's good with numbers, but he's a bit passive. He's not really the type to pick up the phone and shout at people in Iceland."

"Okay, I'll give him a hand."

"Thanks. What about Vinod? Is he still on the case?"

"There's nothing he can do until we get the information back from Iceland. Nigel's got him working on another case in the meantime."

Richard nodded. "I don't suppose there have been any leads from the surveillance on Cullen's family?"

"No, not a sniff."

"Or the girlfriend? What was her name again?"

"Sophie Atkinson," replied Andrew. "No, not yet, but I still think she's our best chance. The police are monitoring her post, home phone, mobile and email. Well the email address we know about anyway. She could have set up other one obviously, not to mention Facebook, Twitter and all that sort of stuff. As you know, they can't monitor her work phone or email without her employer knowing and we don't want to alert them."

"Nothing from any of that then?"

"No. The police look through it daily and then send us the collated material at the end of each week. I'm still getting Vinod to double-check everything when we get it, but it's just the usual stuff. Bills, friends, things she's bought."

"So Cullen's just disappeared off the face of the earth?" Richard asked, shaking his head.

"For now. But he'll make a mistake. They all do."

"I hope so. ZBS have spent a hell of a lot of money with us now and they'll be disappointed if we don't get him in the end."

"We'll get him. It's just a matter of time."

Richard sat forward in his chair. "Anyway, Andrew, that wasn't why I wanted you to come in. I've got another project for you."

"What?" exclaimed Andrew. "What about all the other cases I'm working on? I know Cullen is dormant, but I've got about a dozen others that I'm looking after. I can't take on any more cases."

"Calm down, Andrew. It's not a case. It's a project and I'm going to ask Chris to take on some of your other work."

"What about the Cullen case?"

"You can keep Cullen of course. ZBS wouldn't be happy if I took you off that, especially with this new deal."

"Okay," Andrew sighed. "What do you want me to do?"

"ZBS have an insurance division. They're behind the brand names that you see advertising on the television such as Zebra Pet Insurance, Ruby, who do car insurance for over 50's, iCover.com, who do car insurance for people in their twenties."

"I knew Zebra was them," mused Andrew. "But not the others."

"There are a lot more people making personal injury claims after car crashes these days, because they've heard you can get a few thousand quid if you've got whiplash or you've hurt your back."

"Right …" said Andrew wondering where this was going.

"Obviously those sorts of injuries are difficult for a doctor to disprove – there's no visible injury – so they want us to follow people with suspicious claims and see if the injuries are real. People are wearing a neckbrace when they come into the doctor, but that evening they play five-a-side football with their mates."

"So you want me to follow people who are pretending to have whiplash and see if they're playing football?" Andrew's voice became more disbelieving as the sentence progressed. "You're joking, aren't you? I've got fifteen years investigative experience and you want me to follow people with a bad back."

"Hang on, hang on," Richard said, trying to calm his colleague down. "I don't want you to do the surveillance yourself – I want you to set up the team to do the work. Define the procedures, work out how we're going to do the surveillance reports, recruit the office staff and the investigators and basically get the whole thing set up."

"Sounds like a load of admin to me." Andrew had cooled off slightly, but was obviously still not enamoured with the proposal.

"It's not admin, it's management. You'll head up a team of half a dozen to start with, but that's just for the pilot project. We're going to get a few cases a week for a trial period of three months and, if it goes well, they're going to send all their suspicious claims to us. In a year from now we might need dozens of people and you can be in charge of a whole department."

"It still sounds like a load of admin to me."

"You can do as little administrative work as you like – I need someone like you to design the surveillance procedures that our investigators will follow. And I've employed someone to be your right-hand man to do all the boring admin for you. Well more of a right-hand woman actually. She's been working for ten years in the administrative function of the Northumbia police force and she was running the department in the end."

Andrew shook his head. "So you want me to do a load of admin, follow people with bad backs and at the same time you want me to nursemaid some new girl. Somebody who obviously wasn't good enough to work in the field herself. Sounds like a wonderful job."

"I'm offering you a promotion, Andrew. You're one of my best people and I want someone I can trust to set this thing up for me. We've got to do this by the book as falsified insurance claims can lead to court cases and I can't just take on half a dozen ex-coppers and let them do what they want. We've got to put our own business processes in place that they can follow, with formal paperwork for the client and any follow-up legal work. This could be a lucrative deal for us – there are potentially huge volumes of what is pretty easy work – and of course you should have a share of any profits. That's on top of a pay rise."

"I don't care about the money. My interest is in the investigative work."

"I know you're not motivated by the actual money, but perhaps you could think of it as recognition that I value you. And I'm going to get you to set up the procedures anyway, so you might as well have the money. If you don't want the management role on a long-term basis then just think of it as a six-month secondment to set the team up. You can then return to your original role and your current salary. But you'll still get the profit-related bonus – I want you to feel that you have a stake in the company."

Andrew looked out of the window as he contemplated Richard's proposal. He looked back at him.

"So it's just temporary?" Andrew checked.

"Yes, just six months. We can have a review after three months if you like."

"And if the Cullen case takes off again?"

Richard paused to consider this. "Hmmm, I suppose you can go back to that. That's what ZBS would want anyway. My hope is that it would just be for a week or two anyway and then you would come back to the personal injury team again."

"But only for as long as it takes to set it up."

Richard sighed. "Yes, only for as long as it takes to set it up. I sometimes wonder if I'm actually the boss or just an agent who finds work and then has to sell it to his staff." He laughed to himself. "So have we got a deal then?"

Andrew considered the proposal   .

"Okay," he said, sounding like a sullen teenager agreeing to empty the dishwasher. "Who's this right-hand woman then?"

3. Meetings, Meetings, Meetings. Saundersfoot.
Beginning of April.

"Good morning, Huntly & Meldrum. How may I help you?"

"Could I speak to Sophie Atkinson please?"

"Who may I say is calling?"

"Dan Kernow."

"From …?"

"From nowhere. Look, I've phoned every day for the last week, you must know by now that I'm not phoning from any company. I'm just phoning for a personal call."

The receptionist paused for a second. "Let me see if she's available."

Once again, the telephone system started playing Mendelssohn's Violin Concerto.

The receptionist came back on the line. "I'm sorry she's in a meeting. May I take a message?"

Dan sighed. "May I ask your name please?"

There was silence for a moment as the receptionist considered his question.

"Pavanjit Bhaskar," she replied eventually.

"Pavanjit," said Dan. "That's a nice name."

"Thank you. People normally call me Pav actually."

"Is Sophie really in a meeting, Pav?"

"Of course she is."

Dan thought he detected a slight hesitation before her reply, but decided not to push it. "She has a lot of meetings, doesn't she?"

"They all do here."

"Should I try again tomorrow?"

"Certainly."

"Do you know if Sophie will be in a meeting?"

"I'm afraid I don't know."

"Okay thanks, Pav. Talk to you tomorrow."

4. Right-Hand Man? London. Beginning of April.

It was ten o'clock and Andrew was sitting at his desk in the open plan area of the DHC office. It had been a week since his meeting with Richard and he had spent some of that time looking into the procedures for the new Personal Injury Claim Department.

He looked up as Richard came into the room accompanied by a lithe, slightly-built woman. Andrew judged her to be around thirty years old and perhaps five feet and three inches.

"Andrew, may I introduce Jessica Eadie," said Richard. "Jessica, this is Andrew."

"People normally call me Jess," she said and reached out a hand. Andrew was impressed by her firm handshake and surprised at her strong Geordie accent.

"It's a pleasure to meet you," Andrew said.

"It's good to meet you too, Andy," Jess replied.

"People normally call me Andrew actually."

Jess was slightly taken aback but said: "Pleased to meet you, Andrew."

"Well," interjected Richard, "this will be your desk here next to Andrew. For now, that is. We're sorting out a room upstairs for your team which should be ready in a couple of weeks." He turned to Andrew. "I've been through the high-level plans with Jess just now, but perhaps you two can work out who's doing what between you. Let me know what you decide. I'll leave you to it."

With that Richard disappeared.

Andrew had decided to be hospitable to his new colleague. "Let's get a cup of tea. The kitchen's down this end."

He led the way through the open plan office, introducing her to a couple of people on the way. In the kitchen he switched on the kettle and retrieved a pair of mugs from the cupboard.

"These mugs are normally for visitors but we can use them today. Most people bring in their own after a while. Tea or coffee?"

"Tea, please."

Andrew put a teabag in each mug. "You sound like you're from the north-east," he said.

"Aye, I grew up in Newcastle, well Gosforth to be exact."

"Richard told me you worked for Northumbria police?"

"Aye, for about ten years. I was Head of Corporate Communications for the last 18 months or so."

"Uh-huh," replied Andrew in a non-committal manner. He decided to change the subject before he blurted out what he thought of corporate communications. "What made you want to come down south?"

"I was looking to get out of the police and into a private firm. I saw this job advertised and thought it sounded interesting. As simple as that really. And I thought it might be interesting to see what the fascination is with London."

"It's wonderful if you like being squeezed into small underground trains with ten million other people."

Jess smiled. "Where are you from originally?" she asked. "Your accent sounds slightly Scottish."

"Aye, I'm originally from just north of Glasgow and then Manchester for a while."

"We're both northerners then." Jess said and put her hand on his arm for a second. Andrew almost spilt his tea with surprise at the physical contact.

Jess continued talking. "So what do you think we should do with the Personal Injury Claim Team?" she asked. Andrew was still thinking about her hand on his arm and, before he could say anything, she answered her own question: "The most important thing is to agree an SLA with the client. Don't you think? I'll give them a call this morning and set up a meeting for later in the week. Unless you've already done that?"

"SLA?" Andrew was bemused.

"Service Level Agreement," she explained.

Andrew was none the wiser. "What's that for?" he asked.

"It's a written description of the levels of customer service that they require. Response times for each stage of the process, priority levels, escalation procedures if there is a high-priority case, levels of documentation required. All that sort of thing."

"Sounds fascinating."

"Don't worry, pet, I'll sort it all out," Jess said, placing her hand on his arm once more. Andrew almost jumped again. "I'll arrange a meeting with ZBS and discuss it with them. We'll also need an extranet so that the client can see the progress of each case at any time. I'll sort that out with IT."

"Do we really need that?"

"We want this service to be the best so that they place all their business with us after the pilot project. I'm also thinking that we can provide other services for them and also do the same thing for other insurance companies. We might as well set everything up properly now and it will make things operate more smoothly in the long run."

"Okay …"

"Let's go back to our desks and talk through the rest of it."

She walked off briskly and Andrew hurried to keep up. What followed was an hour of confusion as Jess explained her plans for the new team. He understood all of the words that she used, but not in the way that she assembled them into sentences. It was all "business process analysis", "customer service envelope" and "procedural roadmaps". He felt like a child listening to an adult, but eventually it came to an end.

Jess had allocated ninety per cent of the project tasks to herself, which was good and bad. He certainly didn't want to do any of those tasks himself, but he felt like her assistant, rather than the other way round. Before he knew what he was saying, he had even promised to do his tasks and submit them to her for review by the end of the week.

"So is that all okay?" Jess said, sitting back.

Andrew's head was still spinning and, for about the twentieth time, Jess answered her own question before Andrew could respond. "Good," she confirmed, nodding her head in an encouraging way. "By the way, Andy?" she said.

"Yes?" he replied nervously before realising that she had called him *Andy* again.

"Richard said you were doing another project for ZBS … is it related to this one?"

"Another project?" Andrew was initially confused. "Oh, you mean the Cullen case?"

"Yes that was it, I think. What's it all about?"

Andrew was now on safe ground and enthusiastically launched into an explanation of the case to date.

"Stephen Cullen worked for ZBS and around 18 months ago it was discovered that he had embezzled just over a million pounds from the bank over a three year period. He used the money to pay the medical expenses for his brother's daughter who had a rare illness."

"Oh no, is she okay?"

Andrew looked at Jess. "Yes, she's okay, but that's not the point. He stole money from the bank."

"How old was his niece?"

"I can't remember off the top of my head," replied Andrew, a little annoyed. "Fairly young, one or two years old I think."

"My brother has a young daughter, Andy." She leaned forward and placed her hand on his knee for a moment as she said this. Once again Andrew felt uncomfortable at the contact. "It would be terrible if my niece was seriously ill. It doesn't bear thinking about."

"I prefer Andrew to Andy."

"Really?" Jess said, surprised. "You seem more like an Andy to me." She patted his leg again for emphasis and he felt like a young boy that she was patting on the head. "So have you caught this man?" she asked.

"Er no, not yet. But we will. We nearly had him around nine months ago. Cullen's an intelligent guy and he's only made one mistake so far: he sent a postcard to his brother from north Devon where he was staying. We only heard about it a couple of weeks later but we followed his tracks down the coast to a small place in Cornwall."

"Oh I like Cornwall. I walked the Cornish coastal path a few years ago with my boyfriend before we got married. Where was it that you found him?"

"A small place on the north coast called Trebarwith Strand. Near Tintagel."

"Is that the place with a couple of little shops and the pub that overlooks the beach? What was it called again?"

"The Port William."

"Yes, that's it. We stayed there on our walk. It's a great pub with a lovely view of the beach."

"Yes, anyway," said Andrew, trying to move on, "he was working in the Port William – "

"Actually in the pub?" interrupted Jess.

"Yes, in the pub," said Andrew a little exasperated. "That was just one of the places that he worked. He was very sensible, moving on every few days and always using a different name. He didn't use any credit cards and just worked in pubs, hotels and campsites which often need casual labour. There was never any paperwork because he just worked in exchange for food and a place to pitch his tent."

"So you caught him and then he escaped?"

"No. Yes. Well sort of. We caught up with him at the Port William one night and I had him cornered on a clifftop while I waited for police backup." Andrew then added quickly: "Our role is to locate the individual and then hand the case over to the police to conduct the arrest. Unfortunately Cullen jumped off the cliff before the police arrived."

"Jumped off the cliff? What happened? Is he dead?" she asked. "No, he can't be if you're still looking for him."

"He jumped off a fifty foot cliff into the sea in complete darkness. At first I thought he must have died on the rocks but then I realised he'd landed in the water. Then I assumed he had drowned because he'd told me that he couldn't swim."

"Have you seen any sign of him since?"

"No."

"So he could be dead?"

"No. Not a chance. We never found the body and I found out afterwards that he swam for the county as a teenager. I know the man – there's no way he could have drowned. We believe that he somehow made his way to a train station and left the area. He could be anywhere in Britain now."

"Not abroad?"

"Possible but unlikely. We've obviously got him listed as wanted at all exit points like airports and seaports. Unless I hear otherwise I've got assume he's still in the country."

"So what are you doing to catch him now?"

"There's nothing we can do until he makes another mistake. We're monitoring his credit cards and bank account, mobile phone, family and friends. Also just after we lost him at Trebarwith Strand the bank discovered that he had actually stolen ten million pounds."

"I thought you said earlier that he had stolen one million?" Jess queried.

"That's what the bank told us initially, but then during their annual audit they noticed another nine million that was missing. It took them about a year to notice though. Amazing really."

"And what did Cullen do with the nine million pounds?"

"Nigel, who is our Forensic Accountant – a stupid job title if you ask me – anyway, he's looking into where this nine million went. He's traced it through about five countries to Iceland, but we can't get any information out of them at the moment."

"Are there enough resources on the case?" Jess asked. "I could have a word with Richard."

"Don't worry," Andrew replied irritatedly. "I could ask Richard myself if we needed any more resources. We're just waiting on Iceland at the moment. We've also got a young lad called Vinod Bhardwaj helping out on the case periodically. He's here for a year as part of his degree course and he checks the phone taps, bank account traces, post to family and friends – and he'll help Nigel when he gets the data back from Iceland eventually. I chased things up a couple of days ago and they promised to get stuff to us soon."

"Do you want me to give them a call?"

"No thank you," said Andrew, irritated again. "This is my case. I'm perfectly capable of ringing a bank in Iceland if I need to."

"Okay, I was just offering to help, Andy," she smiled. "You don't need to get your knickers in a twist." Jess patted him on the knee again.

Andrew nodded and was considering apologising for being a little tetchy when she continued: "It's just that I hope the delays in that case aren't going to affect how our client sees our new project."

"Delays!" spluttered Andrew, but before he could formulate a full response Jess stood and said "I'm just going to have a quick word with Richard."

She whisked away, leaving Andrew fuming.

-o-o-o-

Just after seven o'clock that evening Andrew was still working at his desk. Everybody else had now left. He had worked next to Jessica all afternoon but had hardly spoken to her. When she had left for the evening at six thirty Andrew had not even said goodbye.

"Go home, Andrew." He looked up from his work and saw that it was Richard who had spoken to him. His boss had his jacket on and his briefcase in his hand.

"Can I ask you something?" Andrew said. "Can a business-led project management process optimise our strategic core issues?"

Richard paused for a moment and then smiled and said: "Was that just gibberish?"

"Yes, I thought that's what we did now."

"She's good at what she does, you know."

"I think she probably is actually," Andrew replied. "Much as I hate to admit it. I hardly understood a word she was saying though. Well I understood individual words, but not when she combined them into strange sentences. And she seems to think that she's my boss."

"Well you did say that you didn't want to do it," smiled Richard. "And she seemed keen when I was chatting to her this morning."

"Of course she was. She's one of those ambitious types."

"If you want to be the head of the new team just say the word."

"And you know what else? She wants to call the investigators Personal Injury Claim Surveillance Investigators or PICSI's for short. Those big, burly ex-coppers will love being called pixies."

Richard laughed loudly. Still chuckling, he put his briefcase on the desk and pulled up a chair. "That's a good one." He started chuckling again. "My wife will like that one."

"You can't let her call them that," said Andrew.

"Don't worry, Andrew. They won't be called pixies. Not unless you mention it to anyone – if you do, the whole office will latch onto it even if the official name is something else."

"Well, what really annoyed me was that she said that delays on the Cullen case might affect the success of the new project." Andrew used two fingers on each hand to put quotes around the word *delays*. "Like I'm being slow or something."

"Yes, she came in and said the same thing to me. Don't worry, I placated her. I explained that the Cullen case is the biggest case we have at the moment. 'Our flagship case' were the exact words I used. And I explained that the main reason that ZBS were giving us this new work was an investigator by the name of Andrew Muir. They have been impressed by your performance not just on this case but the others you've worked over the years. I told her to keep you sweet because ZBS want you – and nobody else – to set up the surveillance teams."

Andrew looked sheepish. "You didn't tell me that."

"I didn't want you getting any more big-headed. You're a prima donna as it is."

Andrew looked awkward. "And another thing: she keeps touching my arm and patting me on the knee!"

"My wife will like that one as well!" Richard laughed. "I've heard they're friendly up north. Perhaps they're a bit more touchy-feely up there. Or … " – he paused for emphasis – "… perhaps she likes you!"

"In the same way a black widow spider likes her mate before devouring him?"

"Look, Andrew. She's just trying to fit in and, at the same time, she's trying do her best. Can you do me a favour please? Be nice to her. She's good at her job and this company needs people with her skills to move us forward. I'm giving her a percentage of the profits as well, because I want her to benefit if the new team is successful. But I want you to know that you're getting a bigger share, even though you're only on it for a few months. Think of it as a thankyou for the last few years – you were here when we were just a handful of people and you're one of the main reasons why we're doing well at the moment." Richard picked up his briefcase. "Anyway, I'm going home and so should you."

Richard turned to leave.

"Richard," said Andrew. His boss turned back. "I just wanted to say … well, you know … thanks."

"Don't worry about it, Andrew. Just set up a good team for me and then everyone's a winner."

5. Persistence Is A Virtue. Tenby. Mid April.

"Good morning, Huntly & Meldrum. How may I help you?"

"Hi Pav, it's Dan."

"Hi Dan."

"How did the date go last night?"

"I told you it wasn't a date. We just went out in a group."

"Yeah, but you talked to him, didn't you?"

"Yes. He seemed quite nice."

"Good," said Dan enthusiastically. "What does he do?"

"He's just joined a law firm."

"Lawyer, eh? Nice one. Your parents should be happy."

"You're as bad as them. I just happen to mention a boy's name and they ask when I'm getting married."

Dan laughed.

"Anyway," he said. "Is Sophie around today?"

"She's certainly around. I'll give her a try."

Dan listened to the violin concerto.

Pav came back on the line. "Sorry, Dan. She's in a meeting."

"I understand. Well, I think I've tried enough times on the phone now. I believe that's about three weeks I've been bothering you now. I think the time has come to pop over in person and see if she'll talk to me."

"The security guard won't let you come into the office without a pass, I'm afraid."

"I don't suppose you can tell me her home address, can you?"

"I'm sorry, Dan. I don't know it."

"I'll just have to see if I can catch her when she comes out of the office then."

"Well, it's worth a try," Pav said doubtfully.

"You don't sound too optimistic."

"I'm impressed by your persistence, Dan, but I'm not sure if she is. I don't know her that well though. She has only been here a few months."

"Well, it's important for me to actually talk to her. Even if she says she doesn't want to see me again."

"Good luck, Dan. And if it doesn't work out then you can take me out for a drink."

"What about the lawyer?" laughed Dan.

"A girl has to keep her options open."

"There's only one girl for me, Pav. And I'm happy to wait for her if she doesn't say yes this time."

6. Postcard From Wales. London. Mid April.

Andrew burst into Richard's office.

"Another one!" He was waving a sheet of paper in the air. "Another postcard from Cullen. Vinod spotted it. This is a photocopy of it."

"Let me see," his boss said reaching for the paper. Andrew handed it over and sat down in the chair opposite.

"'*Wish you were here, love from Dan*'," read Richard. "Who's Dan?"

"It's Cullen obviously. He used the name Dan Lawrie in Trebarwith Strand."

"How can you be sure? Does the hand-writing match?"

"No, but the last one didn't either. He probably got somebody to write it for him."

Richard looked at the other details on the copy of the postcard and raised his eyebrows in surprise. "It's to Sophie Atkinson."

"Exactly. She knows him as Dan."

"It's to her office address." Richard looked more closely. "It's dated a couple of weeks ago."

"Yes, that's the only trouble. It must have taken a few days to arrive and then the police unit didn't twig that this might be Stephen Cullen when they intercepted it. It's only when they sent last week's batch to us today that Vinod spotted it."

"It's from Tenby. That's in South Wales, isn't it?"

"Yes, Pembrokeshire. According to their website, it's a pretty walled town with a fishing harbour and nice beaches. Looks like he's doing the same thing as last time, working in holiday places along the coast, but this time it's South Wales. I'm going to set off this afternoon if that's okay, Richard?"

"Not so fast. We've got that meeting with ZBS tomorrow morning about our plans for the Personal Injury Claims Team."

"We had a deal, Richard. You said I could work on the Cullen case if it went live again."

"Tomorrow's meeting is important though. We're presenting our plans for how the whole thing is going to work and they expect you to be there to talk them through the actual surveillance. You can set off to Tenby as soon as the meeting is finished."

"But every day wasted is another day he moves further away. We've already lost two weeks."

"That's why I'm thinking one more day isn't critical. Whereas this meeting is very important to us."

"I don't agree," Andrew sighed and shook his head. "But you're the boss I suppose."

"I'm glad you've finally realised," smiled Richard.

"On one condition though," said Andrew. "I'd like to take Vinod with me."

"Vinod?" Richard was surprised. "I thought he was just a kid who didn't know his backside from his elbow? According to you, that is."

"I'll be able to move quicker if I've got someone to help me. He can go round half the pubs and hotels while I do the other half."

"Those are the exact words that I said to you when you said you didn't want him with you." Richard sighed. "Anyway the bank in Iceland have just given us the nod so Vinod's going to be helping Nigel going through all the account data. Sounds like there's load of it to trawl through."

"Nigel can do it on his own, can't he?"

"No way." Richard shook his head. "It was only yesterday that I got budget authorisation from ZBS for both of them to work on it. I'm not going back and telling them it's only going to be Nigel now."

"Is there anyone else who's available?"

"Not at short notice like this. No hang on," Richard said, and paused for a moment before continuing. "I'm not sure if you're going to like this but you can take Jess."

"Jessica? You're joking aren't you?"

"After tomorrow's meeting, ZBS Insurance are probably going to mull over our proposals for a couple of weeks. You know what they're like with something like this. And I'm not going to commit to any more expenditure until they've given the go-ahead. Anyway you said yourself that Jess needs to work in the field, doing some real investigative work."

"Aye, but my suggestion was that she could follow someone who's claiming to have whiplash and see if they still go to their ballroom dancing classes."

Richard ignored Andrew's comment.

"Actually this might work out quite nicely," his boss said, looking up at the ceiling, calculating some figures in his head. "Instead of having you both sitting around for a week or two, I can have you both chargeable."

"There's more to life than chargeable days," Andrew said, exasperated.

"As soon as you tell me that you don't need any salary then I'll forget about how many chargeable days I'm getting out of you each month. Right. You and Jess both come to the meeting tomorrow. As soon as it's finished you can set off. Jess can stay here for another day or so in case there's any follow-up work from the meeting and then she can come over to Tenby after that."

"Great," said Andrew, not looking like he meant it.

"Of course, this all pre-supposes that ZBS sign off on a few days money for you and Jess to go off to Tenby together. I'll give them a call now – why don't you go and tell Jess."

"Great," said Andrew again, as Richard lifted the phone.

-o-o-o-

Jess had always been competitive. She wondered if it was because she had grown up with three brothers, and for some reason she had always tried to out-do them. When they were younger she would often wrestle with them on the floor of the lounge and as they grew older they were always punching each other as they passed in the hall, only playfully but you always had to have your stomach muscles tensed and ready. Jess joined in with all her brothers' games – they often played football in the back garden and she didn't want to just sit in her room playing on her own.

Her eldest brother was Ryan and she was second in line. When he was twelve, Ryan was a quick runner and joined a local athletics club. Jess looked up to her older brother and often came along with their father to when he took Ryan to training. One day, after Jess had been coming along for a few months the coach asked her if she wanted to join the session with the younger age group at the other end of the track. From that first session she was hooked.

Jess had always done well at sprints in school sports days, but after a few weeks the coach realised that she was probably best suited to middle distance running. For the next few years her training was geared to this and by the time she was fifteen she was county 800m champion – and her brother had long since given up athletics.

She trained hard most evenings and improved dramatically over the next couple of years. When she was seventeen, Jess came third in the national junior championships, where most of the runners were a year older. Her coach had high hopes of a win the following year and she was starting to entertain dreams of running professionally when she was older. She even thought about the Olympics but never said it out loud.

While athletics was her main passion, Jess still played other sports at school, including hockey, netball and tennis. She often wondered later whether she should have excluded other all activities and saved herself just for running. Unfortunately one cold winter's day she tore the anterior cruciate ligament in her right knee during a hard-fought hockey match against another school. It was a fairly innocuous collision with one of the girls on the other team, but she went over in a tangle of limbs and felt her knee pop.

The reconstructive surgery was successful and nine months later she was back running, but she was always a few seconds short of where she had been before the injury.

To the untrained eye, she could walk and run normally, but elite performance somehow eluded her. Despite the knee giving her no pain, it seemed that the joint couldn't quite sustain the power that was needed. Or maybe her gait had altered infinitesimally. Her coach wondered if it might simply be the nine months without training and he devised an intense program to rebuild her muscles. However Jess slowly began to realise that she wasn't going to make it and after a year of training she decided to retire at the age of nineteen.

Fortunately her nine month lay-off the year before had been timed perfectly with the run-up to the A Level exams in Sixth Form and she had had plenty of time for revision. With A's in biology and chemistry and a B in maths she had decided to apply to university after her year of dedicated training.

Jess woke from her reverie as she saw Andrew Muir come through the door. I should get back to work, she thought, and stop daydreaming about university and everything else. She turned back to her laptop.

"I don't know if you're going to like this or not," Andrew said as he sat back down at the desk next to hers. "We're going to South Wales."

"Pardon?"

"We've got a lead that Stephen Cullen might have been in Tenby a couple of weeks ago. Tenby is in South Wales."

"Yes I know where Tenby is, but why am I going there? Or you for that matter? We're in the middle of setting up the Personal Injury Claim Team."

"I'm in charge of the Cullen case so I'm going over to South Wales tomorrow and I've just had a meeting with Richard and he suggested that you come out to assist me a day or two later."

"What about tomorrow's meeting with ZBS?"

"I'm still coming along to that," Andrew replied. "However I'm leaving as soon as the meeting is finished. Richard thought that you should stay around for another day or so in case there's any follow-up work from the meeting."

Jess considered the news. On reflection it didn't sound too bad.

"How long might we be away?" she asked after a few seconds.

"I don't know," replied Andrew, shrugging his shoulders. "Could be a few days, could be a few weeks, but ZBS normally just sign-off five days at a time."

"Okay."

Andrew looked surprised. "Really?" He had hoped that Jess might refuse to go.

"Sure. After this meeting tomorrow, we're on pause until ZBS give us the green light. Anyway, I might be able to help you – I know that whole area along the Pembrokeshire coast really well."

"Do you?" said Andrew, surprised again.

"Yes, I went to university in Swansea. It'll be great to go back. So long as I can come straight back here when ZBS approve our plans."

"That's fine by me," said Andrew. "I'm sure Richard will want that as well."

"Okay then," she said, "tell me about this lead ..."

7. Dawn Rage. Tenby. Tuesday. Mid April.

Dan got up at 6.30 in order to catch the early train to London. After three weeks of trying to phone Sophie he wanted to talk to her in person. She may not want to see him again, but he needed to hear that from her in person.

Tenby to London was a four hour train ride, but Dan didn't want to stay the night in the capital unless he really had to. He had therefore decided to set off early so that he could get there and back in a day.

For the last five days he had been working in a beautiful old coaching inn called The Tail Of The Dragon in Tenby. The landlord had looked at him strangely when he had come in the previous week and offered to work only for somewhere to pitch his tent and any leftover food. Fortunately the man was short-staffed that day and he had been prepared to give him a trial. The landlord had then given him the use of a small bedroom that was set aside for staff.

After phoning Huntly & Meldrum the morning before, Dan asked if he might have a day off to visit a friend in London. With five days of working both the lunch and evening shift under his belt, the landlord had decided that Dan's request was fair.

Dan took his bike out of the storeroom at the back of the The Tail Of The Dragon and set off to the station. The roads were nearly deserted at that early hour and he cycled quickly through the centre of Tenby.

Shortly before arriving at the station he came to a set of traffic lights. There was just one solitary car waiting at the red light – a large, new, four-wheel drive BMW – and Dan noticed the letters on the number plate had been placed so that it read R4YS J and he wondered in passing if it was a personalised plate. Or *vanity plates* as they're called in America, he thought to himself with a smile.

Dan slowed for the traffic lights, rolled in front of the BMW X5 and looked left and right. There were no cars in either direction so he decided to just cycle through the junction despite the red light.

He pedalled carefully through the deserted intersection looking both ways carefully and then continued down the road to the station. A few seconds later he heard a car coming up behind him quickly and glanced back to see the BMW bearing down on him. The car sped past him and then screeched to a halt diagonally in front of him blocking his way. Confused, he stopped and looked into the darkened windows of the car.

He watched bemused as the driver jumped out and stormed round the front of the car to stand in front of him. "What the hell do you think you're doing?" the man shouted.

"What do you mean?" asked Dan, confused.

"You went through a red light back there, you stupid idiot!"

"I know I shouldn't have done it, but there were no cars about. It was completely deserted."

"No, it wasn't. I was there. You could have been killed."

"Not really," Dan replied. "You were stationary."

"That's beside the point," yelled the man angrily, jabbing a finger in Dan's direction. "There are traffic lights for a reason. This isn't Italy, you know, where people seem to think that traffic lights are merely a guide."

Dan knew he was in the wrong and, even though he didn't like the man, he decided that the right thing to do was to apologise. After all he was trying to keep a low profile.

"It's early in the morning and I don't think we should get into an argument about this," said Dan. "Let me apologise. I know I shouldn't have gone through the red light."

"You're bloody right, you shouldn't have," the man shouted. "You're an idiot."

"Look, I've apologised. Can't you leave it now?"

"No!" shouted the man, jabbing his finger in his direction again. "You're an idiot and you shouldn't be allowed to ride a bike. You're typical of cyclists who are always bleating about the dangers of cars around them and then you jump onto the pavement to avoid the traffic rules when it suits you."

Dan was too amazed to reply.

"I'm going to report you to the police," the man shouted as he walked back around the front of his car to the driver's door. Dan didn't move and simply watched the man. "Bloody hooligan," was the man's parting shot before he climbed into his car and drove off.

Dan stood there for a second watching him driving away. He shook his head in amazement. Admittedly he shouldn't have gone through the red light, but surely cutting across in front of him and stopping sharply was far more dangerous.

The man didn't know his name so Dan knew that the threat of reporting him to the police was a hollow one, but still he wondered if he should move on from Tenby sooner rather than later. He didn't want to bump into the man again and have the police alerted to his presence.

For now though, he needed to get to the station otherwise he would miss his train.

He jumped back on his bike and set off. The train arrived on time and he climbed aboard for the trip to Paddington. He put the BMW driver out of his mind as he settled into his seat, looking forward to seeing Sophie again.

8. Criss-Cross. London. Tuesday. Mid April.

"How do you think it went?" Jess said to Richard. Their meeting had just finished and they had just said goodbye to the three representatives from ZBS Insurance in reception.

"Fine," said Richard. "They seemed to like it. It's always a good sign when they ask a lot of questions and I think you both gave good answers. I'll give them a call in a couple of days if we haven't heard from them."

"Do you think they'll want to proceed?" Jess asked. Andrew waited impatiently, eager to get off to Wales.

"Don't worry – the pilot project is definite. This review was really just a formality to make sure everyone understands how communications are going to work between the two organisations."

"Is it okay if I head off now then?" asked Andrew, starting to edge towards the door.

"He's got his escape tunnel sorted out and he's raring to go isn't he, Jess?" joked Richard. "Off you go Andrew. Don't forget to send me a short progress report each day and remember that you've got budget for nine man-days, that's five for you and four for Jess. Give me plenty of notice if you want me to ask for some more, but you've got to give me something concrete as a basis."

Andrew hurried back to his desk to collect his bags and then caught a tube to Paddington. He arrived a little time before midday and bought a sandwich with a cup of tea.

He checked the screens for the next departure in the direction of Swansea and found there was a train leaving in a few minutes. Andrew went to the platform, boarded the train and settled into a seat.

-o-o-o-

"The train will shortly be arriving in Paddington," announced the conductor over the train's tannoy. "We apologise for the delay."

Dan stretched and stood to put his jacket on. The man opposite him dropped his Kindle as he stood up and quickly bent to retrieve it, wondering aloud to his wife if he had damaged it. Stupid devices, thought Dan, what's wrong with good old fashioned books that you can touch and feel. They don't break when you drop them. Dan joined the queue at the end of the carriage as the train slid into the station.

The train pulled into Paddington station a little late. Dan stepped down from the carriage and joined the throng of passengers bustling along the platform in the direction of the tube. He glanced at his watch, saw that it was nearly midday and hoped that he was going to be able to reach Sophie's office before she went to lunch.

-o-o-o-

Andrew took a sip of his tea and took a bite of his sandwich as he casually watched the passengers disembarking from the train on the next platform. The train started to move as he took a second bite of his sandwich.

As he chewed the ham, cheese and bread his eyes roved over the people from the other train hurrying about their business. His early years had been in a small village near Loch Lomond and, in fact, all of his childhood had been spent in the countryside so he didn't care for the hustle and bustle of big cities. Crowds of people hurrying from one place to another on their important business reminded him of ants trudging backwards and forwards from their anthill.

The train gathered pace as Andrew took another bite and glanced out of the window again. He almost choked when he saw the man who was walking briskly down the platform just the other side of the reinforced glass. In less than a second the man was past his window and was swallowed up by the crowd.

Had it really been Stephen Cullen? His hair was shorter and a different colour but he was sure it was him.

Andrew turned back and looked at the man sitting opposite him, as if to ask for confirmation that he'd also seen Stephen Cullen. However his fellow passenger had his eyes focussed on one of those stupid Kindle devices and Andrew wondered what the man didn't like about real books that you could touch and feel.

He noticed that the train was emerging from the station and wondered what he was going to do. He stood up, hurried to the end of the carriage and looked at the emergency handle to stop the train. "Alarm - Pull This Handle - Talk To Driver," announced a sign next to a small intercom. "Penalty For Improper Use." Did this qualify as proper use?

He was agonisingly being drawn further away from the man he had been chasing for over a year. Should he pull the handle? Where was the next stop?

He looked back again and saw a conductor at the other end of the carriage. He hurried back down the aisle as fast as he could.

"Excuse me," he said to the conductor, "Where's the first stop?"

"Reading, sir. In twenty five minutes."

"That's useless," Andrew said and walked away, leaving the ticket inspector thinking that life had been so much simpler when he'd worked in the engineering department where he didn't have to talk to grumpy passengers – sorry, 'customers', he thought.

Andrew looked out of the window. He realised there was no point in stopping the train now. They were probably a mile away from Paddington already and even if he did run along the tracks, Cullen would be long gone.

He took out his phone. He rang the office and asked for Jess, but was told that she'd gone for lunch. Why hadn't he got her mobile number?

He rang Vinod who answered immediately.

"Hi Andrew."

"Thank goodness I've got hold of you," said Andrew.

"I'm pleased to hear from you too!"

"I've just seen Cullen and –"

"What? Where?"

"I was just about to tell you. I'm on a train that's just left Paddington. Cullen was on a train that arrived just as my train was pulling out. I can't get off until Reading. Where are you? Can you get over to Paddington?"

"I'm in the office," replied Vinod. "It'll take me thirty or forty minutes to get to Paddington."

"At least. That's no good then. He'll be long gone by the time you get there. Right, my guess is that he's going to see Sophie Atkinson."

"Really? He wouldn't be that stupid, would he? He could be going anywhere. He could be going to see someone from ZBS or his brother could be in town today."

"Maybe," Andrew admitted. "But in my opinion the most likely thing is that he's meeting Sophie Atkinson. I want you to get over to her office straight away. Don't alert her, just wait outside the office and follow her when she comes out. She's working at a company called Huntly & Meldrum, you can get the address from the file. It's not too far from Paddington actually. Right, go. As fast as you can."

"But I'm meant to be helping Nigel …"

"Just go. I'll phone Nigel and Richard and explain what's happening. I'll also phone Billingham at the police unit and see how many men they can spare. They can go to ZBS and other places like Paddington in case he goes back there."

"Okay, I'm on my way."

"You're a good lad, Vinod. I knew I could rely on you. By the way, Cullen's got shorter, darker hair now."

"Okay, I'll text you when I'm there."

Andrew hung up, sighed and sat back in his seat. The train trundled on to Reading at what seemed an excruciatingly slow pace.

9. Well, I Think We Just Ran Out Of Waldorfs.
London. Tuesday.

The offices of Huntley & Meldrum were near Marble Arch and after a brisk fifteen minute walk from Paddington, Dan was sitting on a low wall on the opposite side of the street from the firm's entrance.

Over the next twenty minutes a steady stream of workers coming out of the building and headed off in different directions. Then suddenly there she was, smartly dressed in a grey skirt, matching jacket and high heels. She looked different to the girl he had said goodbye to nine months beforehand overlooking a beach in north Cornwall. That girl had been wearing jeans and a t-shirt, but this was a sharp businesswoman, and he hesitated for a moment. She looked completely at ease in her new life and perhaps being here was a bad idea. No, I've come all this way, he thought, don't give up now. He crossed to follow her as she turned out of the office and started heading towards Oxford Street.

He waited until she was a few hundred yards from the office and then jogged to catch up with her.

"I almost didn't recognise you with your smart clothes on," he said as he came up alongside her.

She turned to glance at him and then stopped when she recognised who it was. "Dan," she said and her face lit up with a smile. "I almost didn't recognise *you* with your new hairdo."

"Blokes don't have hairdos," Dan said. "This is my disguise."

"Not much of a disguise. I would have expected you to be dressed as a seventy year old grandmother or a Japanese businessman or something completely different. Not just looking like a guy who works in a pub, who's decided to cut his hair a bit." She smiled at him fondly.

"It's good to see you, Sophie. Your smile lights up my life, you know."

"What are you doing here, Dan? The police are still after you, aren't they?"

"Yes, but I laugh in the face of danger," he replied deliberately melodramatically. "I wanted to see you, especially as you weren't answering my phone calls."

"I didn't know you'd phoned," Sophie said, with a mischievous grin. "There was this guy called Dan Kernow who kept phoning up though."

"Very funny," Dan retorted. "I thought there might be people listening and I didn't want them to know who I was. But I hoped you might know it was me. And I hoped you would know what Kernow is."

"Of course I know. You can't live in Cornwall for six years and not know the ancient name for the county."

"Why didn't you take my calls then?" he asked lightly.

"I always seemed to be in a meeting when you rang. Very bad timing." She smiled again.

"So I was told by my friend Pav on reception," Dan laughed.

"Ah yes, Pav seems to quite like you. She said that you were coming to see me, but I didn't realise it would be so soon. And she said that if I didn't want you then I should give you her number."

"And I told her that there was only one girl for me. Look, Sophie, how long have you got for lunch? Do you fancy going to a pub or something? I'd really like to talk to you."

Sophie looked at her watch and thought for a moment. "Okay, Dan," she relented eventually. She glanced up the road, thinking of places where they could go. "There's a pub up one of these side streets that we went to on somebody's birthday a couple of weeks ago. It was a nice place. I think it's up this way."

They turned to walk up the road.

"I got your postcard," Sophie said.

Dan grinned. "I was hoping that you would come over to Tenby to see me."

"What was I meant to do when I got there? Were you waiting at the station for me every day?"

"We'd have found each other."

"Oh really," she laughed, "How? Destiny?"

"It works in mysterious ways."

They came to a side street and Sophie paused. "Yes, this is the one," she said and they turned up the road. "Anyway I've got a job now, Dan."

"Yes, congratulations. I'm really pleased for you, Sophie. It looks like a good company from the website."

"It's great. Just what I was looking for. They're a specialist marketing firm with around fifty staff doing projects in all sorts of sectors. I'm working for a client called The FD Centre at the moment: they provide part-time finance directors to smaller businesses who don't want the expense of employing a full-time FD. It's really exciting - they're going places and I'm helping them with marketing the business around the UK and also in South African and Canada next year."

Dan smiled at her enthusiasm. "Sounds good," said Dan, meaning it for Sophie's sake. "Don't you miss Cornwall though?"

"The only thing I miss is maybe Granny Wobbly's Fudge Shop in Tintagel," she joked. "I must have gone there every other day." She stopped and looked up. "Here's the pub."

"Good name," laughed Dan, looking at the sign. "The Grazing Goat. The food must be good with a name like that."

"It's not like the Port William. It's a bit posher – it might be a bit fancy for you actually." She smiled and went in.

Dan followed her into the pub, watching her lithe grace as she walked in and out of the tables and slipped into a seat in the far corner. They carried on chatting while they looked through the menu. He didn't know how to start talking about their relationship – or lack of it – and kept the conversation light.

"Have you had a chance to get back into dancing since you've moved back to London?"

She looked pleased that he'd remembered the passion for dance that she'd had since early childhood and Dan felt that her deep turquoise eyes were looking at him more fondly.

"I haven't had time yet," she admitted, "but someone at work goes to a dance group and I thought I might go along with her at some point."

"What are the people like at Huntley & Meldrum?" asked Dan. "Have you made some good friends?"

"They're okay. Well they're nice. Everybody's very busy and they all live in different parts of London so nobody goes out in the evening together, but I like them, Dan."

"I'm glad you're still calling me Dan. When you left that day you weren't so sure what to call me."

She thought for a moment. "I can't remember your real name – I wouldn't know what else to call you."

"Dan's good. I introduce myself as that these days."

The waitress came over and asked if they were ready to order.

"What's the Salad Of The Day today?" asked Sophie, looking up from her menu.

"Waldorf Salad," replied the waitress.

Dan smiled. Sophie noticed and couldn't help smiling as well.

"I'll have that please," Sophie said and gave Dan a sharp look before he said anything.

"I'll have the Beer Battered Fish & Chips with Mushy Peas please," Dan said, putting the menu back on the table. The waitress left with their order. "You were right about it being a bit fancy for me. Not many pubs have waitresses or a Salad Of The Day. Or those sorts of prices," said Dan. "It is London I suppose."

"Don't worry," Sophie said. "I can pay."

"No, no, I didn't mean it like that. I've got a bit of money saved up."

"Anyway, Dan, how did you find me?"

"Oh, that's a long story," he replied, thinking back. "Well, a few days after I left Cornwall that day, I rang Margaret and she said that you had left and they had no idea where you were. She sounded a little worried actually, but I told her that you'd been saying you wanted to go back to London and get a job."

"I should have told her I suppose, but I just went back home that night in a bit of a spin. It's not often you go out on a first date and the guy tells you he's stolen a million pounds and is on the run from the police. At the start of the evening I'd been starting to wonder if I should stay in Cornwall a little longer, but by the end I just wanted to get out of there."

"Where did you go?"

"I left first thing the next morning and came to stay here in London with an old friend of mine. She was lovely and put me up until I could find a job. And that took quite a while in the end."

"That's why I couldn't find you then. I came to London for a few days at one point because I thought you might be here, but I didn't really know where to look. I was searching in phone books and on the internet for anyone called Sophie Atkinson who lived here. I even phoned a few of them up – they must have thought I was a bit weird. I kept looking occasionally as the months went by and then one day your name came up in Google with a link to the Huntley & Meldrum website."

"Of course. I forgot about that," nodded Sophie. "What a horrible photo though, I can't bear to look at it."

"Nonsense, you look great in it. I can't imagine you looking horrible in any picture."

"Thank you, Dan," Sophie said, slightly embarrassed but pleased about the compliment. She ran her hand through her hair and Dan noticed the light catch the strawberry colouring. "What have you been doing since I last saw you? Actually what did you do during the winter? You didn't stay in a tent, did you?"

"I went back to Cheltenham to see an old school friend and was planning to sleep in his spare room for a couple of nights, but I ended up staying the whole winter." Dan was pleased to keep avoiding the reason he had come to see Sophie, but he knew he was going to have bite the bullet in the end.

"Wasn't that a bit dangerous, going back to see an old friend?"

"Maybe. Probably. But it seemed okay. Anyway I don't think even my parents really knew this guy, we played football together. He's called Tommo. He's got a little place on the edge of Cheltenham and he was great letting me stay there for the winter. I'd have been a little chilly sleeping in the tent."

"Does he know what you did? The whole robbing a bank thing, I mean."

"Oh no. I just told him I'd had enough of the rat race. I went over to visit him for a couple of days and we went out to the pub and met some other old friends. It was great being back in Cheltenham again where I grew up and I just ended up staying a little longer than I originally planned."

"It's good having friends who are prepared to help you that much. I stayed with my friend Emma for about six months in the end."

"Tommo runs his own business as a contract gardener looking after the grounds for local offices and the town council. I helped him on some of his jobs as a way of paying my rent. He was busy in the late autumn so I think I was useful to him, well I hope I was anyway. Then in December and January he worked at a place called the Three Choirs Vineyard about half an hour outside Cheltenham and he got me a job there as well."

"An English vineyard?" said Sophie surprised.

"Yeah there are loads around actually. They were looking for staff because they harvest the grapes in autumn of course and then there's a fair bit to do over the winter turning them into wine. It was really interesting – and the wine was great too!"

"Where are you now then?"

"Still in Tenby, but I think I'll head off soon. Just doing my normal thing of working a few days in each place and then moving on."

"Don't you get tired of it?"

"No, it's great. I'm free to go wherever I want and there are some beautiful places around the country. I'm going to work my way up the west coast over the summer."

The waitress came over with their food. "The Waldorf Salad?" she said. Dan and Sophie smiled again. The waitress placed their food on the table and slipped away.

"So why are you here, Dan? You didn't come all this way just to have lunch with me, did you?"

"Well, I wondered …" Dan looked at his food and speared a chip with his fork, "… if you might want to come and join me?" He lifted his head and looked into her eyes to gauge her reaction. She glanced away.

"I've got a job now, Dan. A good job too. I can't just leave and run away with you."

"Why not?"

"I don't want to spend my life on the run, moving from one place to another. I like having a base, a home, a sofa that I can curl up on and watch the telly."

"But there's never anything good on," he joked and Sophie laughed. He tried again. "Do you want to come over just for a few days? There are some stunning places in South Wales and we can go for walks along the coast and stop in nice pubs for lunch."

"And then sleep in a tent every night?"

"I saved up a bit of money over the winter. We could stay in a bed and breakfast for a few nights if you like. Spend a few days getting to know each other a bit better. I really like you Sophie."

Sophie went quiet and focussed her attention on the salad in front of her.

"I don't think so, Dan," she replied finally. "I can't just take off now. I've only just started this job."

"What about next month? Or the month after that? Or over the summer? You've got to have a holiday at some point."

"I don't know where you'll be."

"I could send you a postcard," he smiled.

"I don't think so, Dan," Sophie said quietly.

A silence descended on the table and neither spoke as they continued eating their meals.

-o-o-o-

At 12.45 Vinod arrived at the offices of Huntley & Meldrum. He sat down on the same low wall where Dan had waited earlier.

He took out a phone and texted "In position" to Andrew.

Before leaving the office he had reminded himself what Sophie Atkinson looked like and now he examined the faces of the women who were leaving the office building. Vinod knew that Huntley & Meldrum only occupied the fifth floor of the tall building and he wondered what other companies had premises there.

Three young men came out wearing jeans and bright shirts, they were laughing and joking. Vinod guessed that they might be graphic designers.

He looked at his watch. 12.50.

Nobody went in or out for a few minutes and then an older woman went into the office on her own carrying a sandwich and coffee in a take-away cup. She had a brisk, purposeful walk and Vinod imagined her to be a manager or perhaps even a management consultant. She reminded him vaguely of a girl he had met at university.That girl was always measured and efficient and he had heard that she was working for a management consultancy firm now.

He looked at his watch again. 1.00pm.

His phoned beeped to announce a text message. It was from Andrew: "Any joy?"

"Not yet," he texted back.

-o-o-o-

Dan and Sophie finished their meal and came out of The Grazing Goat. Standing on the pavement in front of the pub Dan turned to her and said: "Are you sure I can't tempt you to come over for a few days?"

"It's been really good to see you today," she replied, avoiding the question. "It was even nice sitting quietly finishing our meals together."

"I didn't have much choice. Words lack the strength for the weight of message that my eyes deliver."

"Shakespeare or Dan Kernow? Or whatever you're called today."

"Just call me Dan. Anyway that which we call a rose, by any other name would smell as sweet."

"That one I know. Are you saying that your name is Dan Montague?"

"You're avoiding the question."

"I don't want a life on the run, Dan. Bonnie and Clyde was a good film, but I never wanted to be Bonnie. I want a roof over my head and a bed in which to sleep, preferably with electric blankets!"

"You sound like an old woman. Next you'll be wanting a Teasmaid on your bedside cabinet to make you a cup of tea in the morning."

"That sounds good!" she laughed

"So, if I had a house with a bed, a sofa, a telly then you might be tempted to join me?"

"I would," Sophie answered softly. "That would be nice actually. To come for a few days and get to know each other without the fear of someone knocking on the door. And without you looking over your shoulder all the time and me being constantly on edge. But it's not going to happen, is it?"

"It will. It'll just take me a little while to sort it out though," said Dan.

"It doesn't have to be a big house," she smiled.

"I'm in the middle of a few things at the moment. There is of course the long arm of the law that is reaching out for me, but I've also got some other issues that I want to sort out."

"What do you mean?" she asked.

"There are some things that I'm doing for people and I can't leave them unfinished. I'll explain to you one day."

"You're worrying me, Dan. What are you doing?"

"Don't worry. It's all good," Dan changed the subject. "Can I ask you another question? Does it matter where this house is?"

"What do you mean?" Sophie was concerned.

"I don't think there will ever be a chance of me making a permanent base in the UK now, but perhaps abroad. If I can get there. Have you ever fancied living in France or Italy or somewhere like that?"

"Mmmm, that would be okay, I suppose," nodded Sophie. "Paris or Milan or Rome. Sounds nice."

"It might not be this year. Or even next year. I don't know how I'm going to find my way over the channel but I'll work on it."

"I'm not sure if it's enough that you just run away to another country. It doesn't change the fact that you stole all that money."

"Don't you think that I did it for a good reason?"

"Yes, it was a good reason, but it's against the law."

"What if I try and make it right again?"

"How are you going to do that?" she asked.

"I've absolutely no idea, but if I do then do you think there might be a chance for us?"

"I like you Dan, so there's always a chance. I'm not promising anything, but we can spend a few days together and take it from there."

"That's all I wanted to hear," smiled Dan. "I'll let you go back to work, Sophie, but I'll contact you at some point. I've no idea when but I'll get in touch somehow."

He leaned forward and kissed her hard and long. He finally withdrew, but cupped her face in his hands and drank in the sight of her, engraving it in his mind.

"Goodbye, Sophie," he said and released her. He turned and started walking away. She put her hand on the frame of the door to steady herself and then had a sudden thought.

"How will you contact me?" she yelled after him.

He turned his head back as he continued walking, smiled and shouted: "I'll send you a postcard."

-o-o-o-

Vinod had decided he wasn't very good at waiting. It was 1.25pm. He had been waiting for only forty minutes but it seemed like hours.

He glanced up the road and did a double-take. There was a man running towards him and he thought it was Andrew. As the man came closer he realised it definitely was him. Vinod was surprised how fast he was running.

Andrew ran up to him and sat on the wall beside him. He was breathing hard, but not as hard as Vinod had expected after a run from Paddington to Marble Arch.

"Any joy yet?" said Andrew. "Presumably not if you're still sitting here." His breathing was already returning to normal.

"I haven't seen her," replied Vinod. "Do you do a lot of running?" he asked looking Andrew up and down.

"I run between five and ten miles each evening."

"Really? That's a lot. No wonder you seem hardly out of breath. Why didn't you get a taxi though?"

"It took me about seven minutes to run over. A taxi would still be circling round Hyde Park. Anyway, back to Sophie Atkinson – are you sure you didn't miss her?"

"Of course I'm sure," Vinod replied indignantly. "I've missed working with you, Andrew. I'd forgotten what an easy-going person you are!"

"You got here at 12.45, didn't you? Unless you didn't text me straight away."

"That's right. And I did text you straight away."

"It took you forty-five minutes to get over here. She'd probably gone for lunch already."

"You say that like it's my fault the tubes are so slow. I got here as fast as I could."

"Maybe you should have –"

"Hey, is that her?" Vinod interrupted and pointed at a young blonde girl walking towards the office entrance with her head bowed, deep in thought.

"Aye, I believe it is," replied Andrew. They watched her walk up the steps and go into the office building.

"No sign of Cullen," said Vinod, looking in the direction from which she had come. He turned back. "Do you think we should go in and talk to her?"

"I don't think so," said Andrew slowly. "If she is in contact with Cullen we don't want her to warn him that we're around. They might be meeting up again later. If they did meet just now."

"Do you think they did?"

"We've no way of knowing, but Cullen could have got here about an hour ago. It seems reasonable to suspect that Sophie Atkinson came out of the building an hour ago if she's returning now. I think we should assume that they did meet. Now, where would they have met?"

Andrew looked at Vinod, who suspected he was being tested.

"Maybe they went to a pub or restaurant?" Vinod suggested.

"I think that would be the first thing to try. They could have gone for a walk in Hyde Park but she returned from the other direction. They could have gone any number of places, but most people would go to a pub or café or restaurant. They won't have gone far. Not if they went there and back within the hour."

"We could ask around at the pubs at restaurants and show their photos."

"Well volunteered, young Vinod. Obviously start in the direction she came from. Off you go. Call me if you find anyone who recognises them."

"I don't have their photos with me. Have you got yours?"

"I left my bags at the station so I could get here quicker. Why don't you get somebody at the office to text them to you. You can show them to people on your phone."

"That's a good idea."

"And I thought you were meant to be the young high-tech nerd. Off you go then. And start with pubs first – they would do a quicker turnaround at lunchtime."

Vinod stood up. "What are you going to do?"

"I'm going to phone Richard and then Billingham at the police unit and make sure they're doing what I told them to. And whether or not Cullen saw Sophie Atkinson at lunchtime, he will probably do one of two things. He will try and see her this evening or he will go back to Wales. I'm going to make sure we've got someone here, at her home and at Paddington."

Andrew started making his phone calls and Vinod dialled the office number as he set off to hunt for a good local pub.

-o-o-o-

An hour later, Andrew was still sitting on the low wall opposite the Huntley & Meldrum office. He had made all his phone calls and he had decided to remain on the wall until something happened. His nets were cast and he simply had to wait for one of them to twitch.

Andrew was good at waiting. In fact he enjoyed it – it gave him time to think – but he was also happy to clear his mind and just wait.

His phone rang. It was Vinod. A twitch in the nets?

"Hello Vinod."

"I think I've found it. The Grazing Goat on New Quebec Street. That's –"

"Don't worry, I know it. I'll be there in a minute."

He set off briskly and in a few minutes he was there. He went in and found Vinod sitting at one of the tables talking to a waitress. Andrew joined them.

"Andrew, this is Katja." Vinod said.

"Good afternoon, Katja. My name is Andrew Muir. Like my colleague, I work for an investigative agency called DHC," he showed her his identity card. "We're looking for a man called Stephen Cullen. Did my colleague show you his photo?"

"Yes, as I said to your friend, he was here for lunch until an hour ago. His hair is a little darker than in the photo but I think it was him."

"And was he with anyone?"

"Yes, the girl in the other photo your friend showed me."

"Excellent," said Andrew, extremely pleased. "Can you tell us anything about them?"

"He had fish and chips and she had Waldorf Salad."

"Waldorf Salad?"

"Yes, that's the Salad Of The Day today."

"Salad Of The Day?" repeated Andrew.

"Er, yes," said the waitress, a little un-nerved that Andrew was repeating everything she said.

Andrew shook his head. "It's interesting to know what they had to eat, but did you hear anything they spoke about?"

"Not really. A couple of things. I thought that she was his girlfriend, but I wondered if they had had an argument. As I served their food, he was asking her to go to South Wales with him, but she didn't want to go."

"Why not?"

"I think she said she had just started a job somewhere. He seemed a nice boy though and they seemed to like each other. I thought she should go with him. I would have."

"Did you hear them say anything else?"

"No I don't think so."

"Did they leave together?" Andrew asked.

"Yes and I saw them talking in the doorway after they left."

"Okay did you notice anything else about them? Can you tell us anything else at all?"

"No, I don't think so," the waitress said unsurely.

"Okay, you've been very helpful. Could you give my colleague your contact details in case we need to talk to you again please."

Andrew went to wait outside the pub and think about what he had learned from the waitress. When Vinod came out few minutes later Andrew was finishing a phone call.

"I think he's heading back to South Wales now," said Andrew. "I've just called Billingham and told him to make sure his people at Paddington are ready for him. I'm going to head over there now as well."

"Why do you think he's going back there already?" asked Vinod. "They might be meeting up again tonight."

"They left the pub together but he didn't walk her back to the office and she didn't have the body language of somebody who was seeing their boyfriend again tonight. Her head was down and she was deep in thought. Not particularly unhappy … pensive really. If she was planning to see him again tonight, I'd have said that her head would have been up and her walk would have been more purposeful. We'll keep our options open though – I'd like you to wait at Sophie Atkinson's office and follow her tonight just in case."

"Okay," Vinod said but his heart dropped at the thought of sitting on the wall all afternoon.

"But my bet is that he's on his way back now, he might be at the station or he might already be on a train. In which case we can put someone on the train at Reading or further down the line. I'm going to look through the CCTV cameras at the station and we'll see which train he's on. Whatever he does, I think we've got him, Vinod. If he sees the girl again tonight, you'll get him. If he's not left yet, then I'll get him at Paddington. If he's already left then we'll get him picked up down the line. He made a mistake coming here today."

"Okay, do you want me to set off now?" said Vinod. "It's just I haven't had any lunch …"

Andrew rolled his eyes. "It's like working with a small child. Look, grab a sandwich on the way back to Huntley & Meldrum. And get something for later in case you're out all evening, but don't eat it all at once or you'll be sick."

"I'm not really a small child, Andrew."

"I'm not so sure. Call me if you see anything and be ready in case I call you for support."

Andrew turned to go and then turned back. "Did you see the prices in that pub? And what sort of pubs have waitresses and Salad Of The Day? I ask you." He set off for Paddington at a run.

-o-o-o-

At 6.30pm that evening Vinod was south of the Thames in Clapham.

"In position." he texted to Andrew and looked around for somewhere to sit down.

Almost as soon as the text had gone, his phone rang.

"You're at Sophie Atkinson's flat?" asked Andrew.

"Yes."

"And she just went straight home?"

"Yes, she left the office around an hour ago, when I first texted you. Walked to the tube, changed a couple of times and then it was about a fifteen minute walk at this end. She did pop into a corner shop but just came out with a six-pack of bottled water."

"What sort of water?"

"I don't know. Evian I think. Why?"

"You're meant to notice everything, Vinod. Any detail might be important."

"What does it matter what sort of water she buys?"

"Well on this occasion it's probably not important. I was just curious. What's wrong with tap water that's what I want to know. And why do people want to have water shipped halfway around the world when if they really want water out of the ground they can get some from this country."

Vinod was used to Andrew's tirades and changed the subject. "Is there any sign of Cullen at Paddington, Andrew?"

"Do you think I'd have rung you if I'd seen him here? We've looked through the footage on all of the CCTV cameras. Nothing. Anyway, you stay there and call me if you see anything."

Andrew rang off and Vinod was left listening to a silent phone.

-o-o-o-

By nine o'clock Vinod was starting to get cold. He had been waiting outside Sophie Atkinson's flat for two and a half hours. Stephen Cullen was not going to turn up now and he thought about ringing Andrew to announce that he was going home.

He jumped as the phone rang in the silence of the evening.

"Anything?" said Andrew before Vinod had even said hello.

"No."

"I don't understand it. He's disappeared." Vinod had never heard Andrew sounding so unsure of himself.

"Er …"

"What?"

"I don't think he's going to turn up now," said Vinod gingerly. "Is it okay if I head off home?"

"What? No, of course not. Everybody's staying in place until we spot him."

"I'm getting pretty cold here. And hungry."

"Didn't you get some extra food earlier?"

Vinod wished he hadn't brought up the subject. "I've eaten it," he said quietly and held the phone away from his ear ready for another tirade.

"Blithering idiot," was all Andrew said.

"I was bored. Look, I've been on the go since lunchtime – and I did a morning's work in the office before that – can I call it a night?"

"Absolutely not. Cullen's got a limited number of options and we've got to keep looking for him."

"Andrew, London is huge. He could be anywhere. Or he could have left by car or from another train station or by bus or anything."

There was silence for a moment. Then Andrew said slowly: "I think you could be right." Another pause. "Right. Stay there for another hour – I'll get someone to take your place if we need someone to stay there during the night."

"Andrew - " said Vinod, but Andrew had already hung up.

10. Here Be Dragons. Somewhere On The South Wales Coast. Wednesday Morning.

The next morning Andrew was on a train a little way past Cardiff.

He woke with a start as the train came out of a tunnel, sunlight splashing across his face. He looked at his watch. 8.05am. Time to phone his boss and tell him where he was.

"Hi Andrew," Richard Atkins answered the phone after one ring. "Where are you?"

"I'm on my way to South Wales."

"So I hear."

"Really. From whom?"

"Lots of people. I've had voicemail messages and texts all night from various people. Some quite irate. I turned my phone off in the end. What I meant was, how far have you got? Are you there yet?"

"I'm on a train somewhere between Cardiff and Swansea I think. I've got to change in Swansea but I should be in Tenby by midday."

"Tell me all about what happened last night."

"Well," said Andrew. "It was Vinod who gave me the idea actually. He pointed out that Cullen might have left London by another means of transport. We checked the CCTV at the other train stations and then we started with the coach stations. I went for Victoria first and got lucky. He got on a coach at 2pm yesterday afternoon. Unfortunately it was midnight by the time we found this footage and I'd missed the last train. I went to Paddington, slept in the waiting room, picked up my stuff from the lockers and then caught the first train this morning."

"But you can't be sure he's going back to Tenby, can you?"

"The bus he got from Victoria was headed to Bristol and from there you can get a connection to Swansea and beyond."

"Hmmm." Richard wasn't convinced.

"He was trying to cover his tracks by using a different mode of transport on the way back, which was sensible, but he still headed west. He just came to London for a day to see Sophie

Atkinson and I think he was returning to wherever he'd come from. And we know that was Tenby."

"What would you do if you were him?"

"I like his idea of moving from one place to another every few days. I also like the idea of going along the coast where there's plenty of transient labour, especially south-west Wales which is a long way from the big cities. It's quiet but it's not unusual for new people to appear and stay for a few days."

"Hmmm."

"You don't sound convinced, but if we hadn't seen him in London yesterday, I would already be in Tenby. We're simply sticking with the original plan, but I actually think there's more reason to go there now. The fact that he's headed west corroborates the first piece of evidence, the postcard."

"Okay, Andrew, but let me know how it goes."

"He's only 12 hours ahead of me, Richard. I'm going to get him."

His boss paused a moment. "Everyone loves someone who is passionate, Andrew, but not someone who is obsessive. Don't get tunnel vision about this guy. It's just a job."

"I won't get tunnel vision." Andrew sounded offended and Richard could hear that in his voice.

"I'm not so sure. Billingham said you were ordering his guys around and I heard you forgot about Vinod last night."

"The blithering idiot waited until one o'clock in the morning to phone me to ask if he could go home," said Andrew plaintively.

"How surprising that he left it so long. And you so approachable."

Andrew didn't say anything.

"All I'm saying is remember to apologise to him," said Richard.

"I was going to get someone to take over from him well before midnight, but I forgot with all the other stuff going on."

"Just say sorry. He'll get over it. And take your nose away from the grindstone sometimes. Not too much because you're good at what you do, but just occasionally look at the people around you."

"Okay, okay."

"And another thing," Richard added. "I'm sending Jess to help you as we agreed. Probably tomorrow morning. Look after her. Get her to help you, but look after her."

"Yes, sir," Andrew said sarcastically.

"I like that. You should call me sir all the time. I'll pretend you weren't being sarcastic. And another thing."

"How many more things are there?"

"It's just you and Jess. Don't call in loads of other people like you did yesterday. You had half the Metropolitan Police running around like idiots and, what's worse as far as I'm concerned, about six of our staff. And I can't charge for their time because I didn't get it signed off by the client beforehand."

"We had Cullen in our sights and we had to react quickly."

"That's fine once in a blue moon," said Richard. "But don't make a habit of it. We've got other projects and we've got budgets. Down in Tenby it's just you and Jess. And you're lucky I'm giving you Jess."

"I'm not sure if lucky is the right word."

Richard laughed. "It's like a scientific experiment I'm conducting. Put the two of you in a closed environment for a week and see whose personality gets modified the most. I would put my money on Jess re-shaping you, but you're pretty intransigent."

"I take that as a compliment."

"Have fun, Andrew. You never know, you might actually enjoy yourself. And don't forget to send me a report at the end of each day. Bye for now."

Andrew said goodbye and they hung up. He looked out of the window at the world going by and shook his head. He certainly was not going to enjoy working with that patronising, ambitious woman.

11. Funny Feeling. Tenby. Wednesday Morning.

While Andrew Muir was trying to doze off again on the train, Dan was cycling through Tenby.

He had arrived back the previous evening and gone straight to the The Tail Of The Dragon. Upon his return he had announced that he was moving on the following morning – and the landlord had almost kicked him out on the spot. However Dan had apologised profusely and offered to work the remainder of the evening. This offer had been accepted grudgingly when the landlord remembered that someone else had phoned in sick.

Dan had enjoyed his last night's sleep in the bed at the top of the pub and wondered if he'd be sleeping in the tent for the next few days.

It was a shame to leave Tenby but the altercation with the BMW driver early the previous morning had worried him. He didn't want to bump into the man again and be reported to the police.

And for the few hours that he had been in London he'd had a funny feeling of being watched. He hadn't actually seen anyone following him, but he resolved to play it safe and move on. In addition he felt it wise to move a good distance along the coast.

A few days previously he had been talking to one of the regulars in the pub and they had mentioned a small town further along the coast called St Davids. Dan had thought it sounded ideal. Wales' largest cathedral in Britain's smallest city, the man had said proudly of the place where he had grown up. St Davids was more of a large village as it only had half a dozen streets and a population of two thousand, the man had continued, but pilgrims had been coming to the final resting place of Wales' patron saint for over 1500 years.

What appealed to Dan though was its location as the most westerly point of Wales and the fact that it was a popular destination for watersports enthusiasts and tourists wanting to see the wildlife of the Pembrokeshire Coast National Park. He hoped that the place might be remote enough to hide for a while, whilst being busy enough that he might be able to find some work.

However St Davids was around forty miles further up the coast – and he didn't want to arrive too late or it would not leave him much time for finding a job. Instead of cycling as he normally would, he had decided to take the bus.

Dan arrived back at the coach station – where he'd arrived from London twelve hours earlier – bought a ticket and loaded his bike on the bus.

The bus arrived in St Davids mid-morning and he climbed down the steps and unloaded his bike. He looked around as the other passengers disembarked and filtered away into the village. St Davids was as small as he'd expected, but he liked the feel of the place with its slate buildings and the relaxed pace with which people were sauntering around the high street. The town reminded him of Tintagel in northern Cornwall where he had been the year before: in addition to the slate stonework, the buildings had the same sash-windowed, double-fronted architecture.

Despite the town's modest size there were perhaps twenty shops and maybe the same number of hotels, pubs and cafes. He felt that he should be able to find somewhere to work.

Noticing a bakery on the other side of the street, he realised that he hadn't yet had breakfast. He walked over to the shop and joined the queue.

"Do you sell croissants?" he asked when he arrived at the head of the queue.

"Do you think you're in France, boyo?" smiled the large lady who was serving him. "We don't get much call for fancy things like croissants here. How about some bara brith?"

"What's bara brith?" Dan asked.

"Welsh tea cake. The name means speckled bread. Delicious, it is. People normally have it at teatime, but I thinks it's nice for breakfast. I'll even spread some butter on it for you."

"Okay I'll give it a go," said Dan, getting his money out. "By the way, I'm looking for work for a few days. You don't need any staff here, do you?"

"I'm lucky to have a job here myself and I don't want any competition from the likes of you," she joked.

"I don't suppose you know of anyone else looking for staff, do you? I only want to work here for a few days, but I'm happy to work for nothing really, just in exchange for a bit of food and somewhere to pitch my tent."

"You are competition. Even under-cutting us, you are!" She turned to the woman who was behind Dan in the queue. "Did you hear that Bethan? Cheap labour – you're not looking for anyone, are you?"

"I was just about snap him up," replied the woman. "That's exactly the sort of price I can pay."

Dan turned to look at the person who was smiling at him engagingly and was immediately struck by her athletic looks and long auburn hair. He judged her to be in her mid-thirties and she was almost as tall as he was himself.

"Hi, my name's Bethan," the woman said, shaking his hand. "I could do with someone to help out today. In about an hour's time actually."

"That's great. I'm your man."

"I haven't told you what the work is yet."

"That's fine. I'll do anything. Cleaning the toilets, taking out the rubbish, washing up, whatever."

"Why don't you come back to my office and I'll tell you about the work and you can tell me about yourself," she suggested.

"That would be great," said Dan, happy to have found an opportunity so quickly.

"And your first task is to carry some of this bread for me please." Bethan pointed at a large pile of loaves that were being loaded into carrier bags on the counter by another of the shop assistants. "Can you grab a couple of bags?"

"Sure," said Dan. He paid for his bara brith, pushed it into his pocket and picked up two of the bags.

"Thanks, Zena," said Bethan and she turned to leave.

Dan followed Bethan out of the shop and grabbed his bike that was leaning against a lamppost outside. He carried the two large bags of bread in one hand and pushed his bike with the other.

"Zena's an unusual name, isn't it?" asked Dan. "She sounded Welsh to me."

Bethan laughed. "She only says 'boyo' for the tourists. Mind you, she's as Welsh as me. We both grew up here but her parents are German and mine were Scottish." She glanced at him. "So what's your name then?"

"Dan."

"Pleased to meet you, Dan," she said. "This is my place here."

They turned into a gateway with a sign proclaiming that this was Alun House, the home of Geddes Outdoor Sports. As they walked up the gravel driveway Dan saw that it lead to a large Victorian house built from the same slate as the other houses in St Davids. It looked like two small wings had been added to the main house some time after it had been built and Dan judged that the building must have around a dozen rooms. The house was set in grounds that stretched a hundred yards in each direction and a number of large trees were scattered around the gardens. A low stone wall bordered the property.

"Nice place," said Dan as they approached the house.

"It is," agreed Bethan, "but it soaks up money. Heating, decorating, anything costs a lot of money. Let's go into the office and I'll tell you all about what we do."

Dan leant his bike against the front of the house and they went in through a large open doorway.

Bethan lead him into a room that was on the right hand side of the hallway and she put her bags on the floor by a large old oak desk.

"Put your bags down there as well and grab a seat." She said as she flopped into a chair behind the desk.

Dan did as she had suggested.

"Geddes Outdoor Sports was started by my parents about twenty five years ago," Bethan began. "My dad was a climber and my mum was into kayaking. They came here on holiday before I was born, really liked the place and decided to settle down here. They worked in pubs and on campsites for a few years and then decided to set up their own business."

"Are they still involved in the business?"

"No, I run things now," she said. She paused and then continued: "My parents died a couple of years ago."

"I'm sorry to hear that," Dan said, regretting having asked. He moved the conversation on quickly: "What sort of things do you do here?"

"Climbing, kayaking, kiteboarding, coasteering. And we also organise educational programmes for schools with coastal walks, boat tours to see the seals and other local wildlife along the coast, team building events and that sort of thing. We've got half a dozen full-time staff and some local climbers and kayakers who help out occasionally."

"Sounds great," said Dan, thinking that this was going to be an excellent job.

Bethan paused and looked at him closely. "So are you serious about working for just food and lodging?"

"Absolutely," said Dan. "Just somewhere to pitch my tent will be fine."

"We run a campsite about five minutes away, but you can stay here in Alun House if you like. We've got a couple of spare rooms upstairs. Nothing luxurious, but they've got decent beds."

"That would be nice, but I don't want to be any trouble."

"It's fine. And then you'll be right here if we need you to do anything. Also, we normally have a fair bit of food available as we include lunch or dinner with some of the packages. I'll show you the kitchen in a minute and you can just help yourself whenever you like."

"That's great," said Dan.

"But," she warned, "you can consider today a trial. If it goes okay then you can stay until the end of the season if you like. And by the way, I really appreciate the fact that you don't want any money – that would help with cashflow right now as it's early season and we're pretty quiet – but if you stay for the busy summer period then I'll be happy to pay you the going rate."

"That's kind of you, but I was only planning to stay for a week or so."

"Why just a week?" she asked.

"I'm touring round Wales. I was working for a few days in Tenby and somebody said it was nice here."

"It's beautiful here, Dan. I think it's the loveliest corner of the world."

Dan nodded. "So what do you need me to do today?" he asked.

"We've got a group coming in to do coasteering. Do you know what that is?"

"Not really …"

"Some parts of the coast round here are fairly rocky, with low sections of cliffs. We take people along a mile or two of the coast in wetsuits and they scramble across rocks, jump into the sea, swim along, climb up some more rocks, jump in again."

"Sounds fun," Dan said.

"We've got some groups coming in for other things as well, but the coasteering party only has one instructor at the moment and we need at least two for a group this size. I was about to go out with them myself but I really need to man the office. So it's good that you're here. By the way, have you done climbing or kayaking? Do you have any qualifications in those sorts of things?"

"No, I'm afraid not."

"That's okay, I wasn't expecting it. Anyway the second instructor for coasteering only needs to be there in case there's an accident. And there are no official qualifications for coasteering anyway." She glanced at him. "You can swim, can't you?"

"Oh yes," Dan smiled. "I swam for the county when I was a teenager."

"That's great. Anyway over the next few days you can help with the menial stuff if that's okay. You can't take classes obviously, but we need drivers and somebody to run errands occasionally. You can drive, can't you?"

"Yes," Dan nodded.

"Okay," said Bethan, standing up. "Let me show you the kitchen and then our common room at the back of the house. And I'll introduce you to the boys."

"Great," said Dan, standing up. "Thanks for the job, Bethan. It sounds perfect."

"Don't forget, today is just a trial. By the way, what's your surname?"

"Er … Adamson," he stuttered. "Dan Adamson."

"Okay, follow me." Bethan lead the way to the kitchen across the hall and then through to the back of the house. They went upstairs and she showed Dan his bedroom. It was a plainly decorated boxroom, but, as promised, the bed looked comfortable.

They went back downstairs and Bethan lead him into a lounge. There were four men in their twenties in the room and Dan was surprised to see that one of them was crouched on the floor with his hands by his ankles looking like he was about to leap in the air.

The young man looked over as Bethan and Dan entered the room and then stood up sheepishly.

"Still trying to reach the ceiling, eh Bez?" smiled Bethan. The other three lads laughed and Bez looked embarrassed. Dan looked up at the ceiling. Being an old Victorian house, the ceiling was quite high.

"Anyway, Dan, this is Bez. Gareth Berriman, but we call him Bez." Dan shook hands. Bez was about his height and well built. He was in his late twenties with short-cropped hair.

"This one's Kermit," continued Bethan, "and this is his older brother Donkey or Donk for short. Their real names are – actually it doesn't matter what their real names are. And this is Ciaran MacGwyverdine. Dan's going to be working with us for a few days, boys – and he's your second today, Ciaran. Make him a cup of tea or something, will you? Today's groups should be arriving soon – I'll give you a shout in about ten minutes."

Bethan turned to leave the room, then turned back. "By the way, there's four children in this party today, Ciaran. So best behaviour."

"That's okay, Beth, I like children," said Ciaran, then paused for effect. "I couldn't eat a whole one though."

"Oh no," said Bez, putting his head in his hands dramatically. "He says that every time."

Dan shook hands with his new colleagues as Bethan left the room shaking her head.

"Kettle's over there, Dan," said Bez, pointing at a small table in the corner of the room. "You can get water from next door if it's empty. Milk's in that little fridge underneath the table."

"Thanks, Bez," said Dan and started to walk over to the kettle.

"Hang on a minute," said Ciaran, holding out his hand to intercept Dan. "We were just having a little competition to see if everyone here can touch the ceiling. I'll go first." Ciaran was tall and slender and jumped easily to touch the ceiling with the palm of his hand. Dan judged that the ceiling was over nine feet high.

Kermit and his brother were next. They jumped up and touched the ceiling effortlessly but only with their fingertips. They looked at Dan.

"Okay," he shrugged and jumped smoothly to touch the ceiling with his fingertips as well.

All three of them turned to look at Bez with broad, expectant grins. "That's all of us then," said Ciaran. "Oh no, hang on, you haven't done it, Bez."

"Yeah, yeah," he said. "Very funny."

"Go on then."

Bez crouched down as low as he could and then with a huge shout he leapt in the air. Veins were standing out on his neck due to the strain and he stretched his arm as far as he could – and stretched a little further still – but his grasping fingers missed the ceiling by quarter of an inch.

"Oh, you nearly got it that time, Bez," Kermit shouted and they all laughed. "Have another go."

Once again, Bez bent down and sprang with all his might. His flailing hand narrowly missed the ceiling once more.

"You almost left the ground that time, Bez!" guffawed Ciaran and all three of the boys fell onto the sofa laughing. Ciaran turned to Dan. "The funniest thing is that he gets *so* close every time!"

Bez took off again, with the same extremely close result. Dan looked at Bez and couldn't work out why he couldn't reach the ceiling. He was the same height as Dan was himself and he had made the jump quite easily.

"The other funny thing," said Ciaran as Bez launched himself once more, "is that he keeps trying."

"And that he tries *so* hard!" laughed Kermit.

"It takes a lot of force to lift something that big though," retorted Ciaran. "He has his own gravitational pull after all."

Dan made himself a cup of tea while Bez kept on trying to reach the ceiling. Crouch, hands by ankles, pause, launch. By the time his tea was made, Bez was red-faced and out of breath. Dan sat down in an armchair and Bez sat down in another chair alongside him.

"What was your name again?" asked Bez.

"Dan."

"Pleased to meet you, Dan." Bez was still breathing heavily. "This is the only thing they can beat me at, you know. I'm the best at everything else."

"I'm sure you are," smiled Dan, sipping his tea.

"So where did Bethan find you then?"

"In the bakery over the road."

"Really? Just standing there minding your own business, were you? That sounds like the boss – she'll press-gang anyone."

Dan smiled. "She seems like a nice boss actually."

"Yeah, she's not bad I suppose," said Bez. "And you should see what she looks like in a wetsuit!"

"I'm more interested in seeing her when she takes the wetsuit off," said Donk.

"She's pretty hot for an oldie," said Kermit, who looked like he was only twenty. "She must be like thirty five or something. What do you think, Dan? You're that era, aren't you?"

"'Fraid so." Dan replied, sipping his tea.

"No way, man," said Kermit, his eyes widening. "What's it like being that old?"

"It's great," Dan laughed. "What's it like being a small baby?"

"Nice one, Dan," shouted Bez and tickled Kermit under the chin saying "Coochee-coo."

"Look what you've started now, Grandpa," Kermit shouted at Dan, knocking Bez's hands away from him.

"Where you staying, Dan?" asked Ciaran, while Kermit and Bez kept fighting.

"Here," replied Dan. "Bethan said I could stay in a room upstairs."

"Really?" said Ciaran. "Upstairs with Bethan. Wow."

"Does she live here herself?"

"Course she does. This is her place. It'll just be the two of you tonight."

Dan didn't know what to make of this information, but the boys continued to make ribald comments at his expense.

He was saved a few minutes later when Bethan called them to take their groups out for the day.

12. Little Town Of The Fishes. Tenby. Wednesday Midday.

Andrew stepped down from the bus and looked around.

He had understood that the town was a fair size but he was disappointed by the huge number of pubs, hotels, chip shops there were in Tenby. And that was before he considered all of the other retail outlets: newsagents, sweet shops, souvenir shops and so on. He decided that the place must be very busy in summer to support this amount of trade.

Andrew wondered where to start.

He went into a newsagent and bought a streetmap of Tenby. While he was there, he showed the photograph of Stephen Cullen, but the shopkeeper had not seen him. He came out of the shop to sit on a bench to look at the layout of the town and decide on his plan of attack. The legend in the top right corner declared that the Welsh name for the town was *Dinbych-y-Pysgod*, meaning *little town of the fishes.*

Cullen could be working in pretty much any of the hundreds of buildings in the town centre. Every one was a candidate.

He decided to start with the street that he was in right now and work his way to the seafront. And then cover all the other areas of town. He would ask in every shop, hotel and pub on a road and then mark that road off on the map.

This was going to be a long day. The journey of a thousand miles begins with a single step, he said to himself. There was a Sainsbury supermarket over the road and he decided to start there.

-o-o-o-

Three hours later Andrew Muir finally struck gold.

He had only crossed off half a dozen streets of the thirty or forty that formed Tenby town centre when he went into a pub called The Tail Of The Dragon.

"Excuse me," said Andrew to the middle-aged man that was behind the bar. He held out the photograph of Stephen Cullen. "Have you seen this man?"

The barman glanced at the photograph and then looked more closely. "My God, yes that's Dan." He looked up at Andrew, narrowed his eyes and suddenly looked worried. "Why? You're not from Customs & Excise are you?"

"Firstly, HM Customs & Excise don't exist any more. They merged with the Inland Revenue in 2005 to become HM Revenue & Customs." Andrew was always a stickler for detail. "Secondly, why are you so concerned? Do you think that you might have been doing something illegal?"

"Er, no, of course not."

"Good. Well, if you can help me find this man then I won't mention this conversation to my friends at HMRC. Does this man still work here? This man you know as Dan."

"No, I kicked him out this morning. I knew he was trouble. Well not at first. In fact he was good as gold for the first part of the week and then he comes back yesterday and says that he's leaving."

"Really?" said Andrew. "What reason did he give?"

"Just said it was time he moved on. Very annoying I can tell you. He was just about the best person who's ever worked for me. Really quick, good with the customers, worked long hours. He did say he wasn't going to stay long, but I was hoping he might change his mind."

"So he just said he wanted to move on. No other reason?"

"No. Just that it was time to go. And after I'd given him the day off to visit a friend in London as well. He got back here at eight-ish last night and then announced he wanted to leave today. I almost kicked him out there and then, but the thing was, I needed him to work yesterday evening and I said he could stay the night. He left at about eight o'clock this morning."

"Do you know where he went?"

"Not a clue. I asked him where he was going, but he just said along the coast."

"Did he say which direction?"

"No, he didn't say, but I saw him when he was leaving on his bike and he turned right out of here."

"So if you were going along the coast, which way would you be going if you turned right out of here? Where would you be heading for?"

"Saundersfoot direction I suppose. But he could easily have turned left at the top of the road and gone off Penally way."

"What was he wearing when he left?"

"Er, jeans and a blue fleece."

"Does he look the same as this photograph?"

The man glanced at the photo again. "Sort of. His hair's a bit shorter than the photo. And darker. A bit."

"But you're sure it's him."

"Oh yes, that's Dan." The barman thought for a second. "You said earlier that I called him Dan. Like his real name's something else."

"I don't think that's any of your concern considering you've been harbouring a fugitive from justice."

"I knew it!" said the man, banging the top of the bar with the flat of his hand. "I knew there was something funny about him. Wait 'til I tell my wife."

"What sort of bike was he riding?"

"No idea," he replied, shrugging his shoulders. "I'm not into bikes. It was blue."

"Blue. That's very helpful, I must say."

"Oh, good."

"I was being sarcastic," said Andrew shaking his head.

"Oh."

"Is there anything else you can tell me about him?" asked Andrew.

The man thought for a moment. "Er, no, not really."

"He worked here for a week and you don't know anything else about him?"

"He liked corn flakes for breakfast," the barman said hopefully.

"That piece of information could be vital."

"Oh, good," said the man, and then looked at Andrew's face more closely. "You're being sarcastic again, aren't you?"

"Yes. At the risk of exposing your lack of knowledge still further, what surname was he using?"

The man looked up at the ceiling, his face a picture of concentration. He scratched his head. "Hang on, I can get this." He looked down at the floor, his shoulders slumped and he looked up sheepishly at Andrew. "No I can't remember. It was something Scottish."

"He worked here for a week and you don't know his name." It was more of an accusation than a question. "Can you help me in any other way?"

"Oh yes, I've remembered something else," said the man excitedly and then instantly became wary. "You won't be sarcastic again will you?"

"Of course not. You've been so amazingly helpful so far."

"I won't tell you if you're going to be like that," said the barman petulantly.

Andrew didn't say anything but looked impatiently at the man.

"Are you interested in knowing what football team he supports?" the barman asked cautiously.

Andrew thought for a moment. "Actually I am," he replied.

"Leeds," the man said proudly. "They beat Cardiff at the weekend – that's my team, so we were having a chat about it. Three-one it was. Did you see it? Richardson got sent off for what was a perfectly good tackle. In my day we'd have slapped him on the back and said well done. And now you get a red card for it."

"May I see his room please?" Andrew got the conversation back on track.

"His room?"

"You said he stayed here."

"Oh yes, I let him kip in the attic room. I'll just get the wife to look after the bar and I'll take you up."

The man shouted up the stairs and presently his wife appeared. Andrew was taken up two flights of stairs and shown into a small room with a vaulted ceiling. There were no pictures on the walls and no curtains on the tiny window in the gable wall at the end of the room. There was simply a chair and a bed, on which were some folded sheets and blankets.

"Has the room been cleaned since he left?" asked Andrew curiously.

"No," replied the man. "It looks like he's stripped the bed and folded the sheets for us. He's a good lad."

"Your opinion of this man seems to be quite variable."

The landlord didn't know what to answer to this.

"Okay," said Andrew. "I was hoping he might have left some clue as to his next destination. A leaflet or something like that. Oh well."

"In the films they normally find a book of matches," the man said helpfully.

"Yes, I imagine they do." Andrew looked under the bed but there was nothing there. "What did he do when he wasn't working downstairs."

"I've no idea really. He would just sit up here and play on his computer."

Andrew looked surprised. "He has a computer?"

"Yes, a laptop. Looked quite smart. I've just bought a new laptop but his was much fancier than mine. He told me that it was 16 gigabytes. Or was it megabytes?"

"Do you have WiFi here? Could he get on the internet?"

"Yes, I gave him the number thingy to use the broadband."

"Okay, you've actually been quite helpful there." Andrew turned and left the room. The man looked pleased and then hurried to catch up.

As they walked back downstairs Andrew thanked him again. He gave the man his business card and asked him to call if he remembered anything else. As he was about to leave, Andrew turned back and asked: "How long would it take to get to Saundersfoot?"

"About twenty minutes by car, I would say."

"Is it a big place? How many shops and pubs and hotels?"

"Oh not many."

"Less than Tenby?"

"Oh yes a lot less."

"Okay. Thank you. Do you know where I could hire a car?"

The man gave him directions and Andrew set off briskly. If he was quick he could pick up a car and get round most of Saundersfoot before the end of the evening. He was only a few hours behind his quarry and if luck was on his side then he might just catch up with him.

Five hours later Andrew's hopes had dissipated. He walked dispiritedly out of a pub on Saundersfoot harbour called The Captains Table. After asking in nearly every establishment in the village, he had finally come to this friendly pub only to discover that Cullen had worked here ten days ago. Andrew realised he had picked the wrong direction along the coast. His quarry was heading west not east.

Andrew looked at his watch. Eight thirty. He decided to call it a night and find somewhere to sleep. In the last thirty-six hours he had only slept fitfully in Paddington station and on the train. It was time to rest and he would start searching west of Tenby in the morning.

He walked back to where his car was parked which happened to be near a comfortable looking guesthouse, The Gower Hotel. He breathed a sigh of relief when they said that they had a room available and he checked in.

Andrew asked for a sandwich with a pint of bitter to be brought up in half an hour and he climbed the stairs to find his room. He sent a quick email to his boss, Richard, with a short report about his day and then phoned Vinod.

"Hi Andrew," Vinod answered cheerfully. "Or should I say 'Andy'?"

"Hello Vinod. I prefer Andrew actually."

"I was speaking to Jess this afternoon and she called you Andy all the time. Andy this, Andy that. She seems to be on very familiar terms with you."

Andrew sighed. "I told her a few times that I prefer to be called Andrew. Andy seems like a younger person's name."

"And you're an old person, aren't you? An old person in a middle-aged man's body."

"Vinod, I was just phoning up to see if there have been any developments on tracing the money?"

"Well as a matter of fact, the answer is yes."

"Really, well why didn't you phone me?"

"We're still going through it actually. We're still in the office."

"Who's we?"

"Nigel, me and Jess. And it's Jess you've got to thank. She rang the bank in Iceland yesterday afternoon and gave them a kick up the backside. And then miraculously they've sent over thousands of transaction logs today. The three of us are going through it trying to find all the payments that went over there to various accounts from the African accounts. And here's the interesting bit, it's starting to look like all the money that got spread around in hundreds of accounts then came back to half a dozen accounts in the UK."

"And then where?"

"We don't know yet – we're going to try and get access to those accounts tomorrow. Nigel thinks that they're probably ZBS accounts though so it should be okay."

"So he sent the money around the world and then back to ZBS again?"

"It looks like it," agreed Vinod. "So how have you got on today? I guess we'd have heard if you'd caught up with him."

"I was so close Vinod. I arrived in Tenby at midday and found out he'd left at about eight o'clock. Something must have spooked him because he decided to leave the place where he'd been working, but I think he's still in south Wales somewhere."

"Why's that?"

"He told the man for whom he worked that he was moving along the coast. Obviously he could have left the area, but why come here back here at all if that was the case?"

"I see what you mean. Unless he came back for something?"

"It's possible, but I think he travels fairly light in case he needs to make a run for it. Anyway I've got to assume that he's in this area and exhaust all the possibilities. Unfortunately I picked the wrong direction along the coast this afternoon. I came to a place called Saundersfoot which is east of Tenby, but he was here ten days ago. I should have gone west – that's more logical anyway."

"Why's that?"

"I'm thinking he started in Cardiff and then he's working his way along the coast westwards. Anyway I'll try some places the other side of Tenby tomorrow."

"Andrew, Nigel's just given me a funny look," Vinod said. "I think he wants me to go and help if that's okay."

"Sure Vinod." Andrew hesitated a moment. "Actually there was just one other thing."

"Yes?"

"I just wanted to say … well, I just thought I should say sorry. For leaving you outside Sophie Atkinson's place until past midnight last night."

There was silence down the line. Vinod didn't know what to say to this at first. Then he recovered himself. "That's alright, Andrew."

"I appreciated you acting quickly yesterday lunchtime when I asked you to help. It was a relief to call someone and have them respond immediately. That's exactly what you want in a situation like that. So I'm sorry you were there so long without me sorting out a replacement."

"That's okay. It was no big deal, honestly." Vinod was starting to get embarrassed now. Pleased but embarrassed.

"Right," said Andrew, who was uncomfortable himself. "Give me a call tomorrow if you find out what happened with the money."

"Will do boss."

"Bye Vinod."

"Bye Andy," Vinod said with a laugh and hung up before Andrew could say anything.

13. Cheese And Pickle Sandwich. St Davids.
Wednesday Evening.

At ten o'clock that evening, Dan went into the kitchen of Alun House which doubled as Bethan's home and the office of Geddes Outdoor Sports. Dan hadn't seen Bethan since he'd got back from his day assisting Ciaran with the coasteering group and he'd spent a few hours in his room, but now he'd decided to look for something to eat in the kitchen.

As he was looking through the fridge he heard the front door open and glanced over to the door of the kitchen as Bethan appeared.

"Hi, Dan," she said. "How's it going?" She started filling a kettle with water.

"Not bad thanks. I was just going to get a cheese sandwich if that's okay?"

"Sure, help yourself. Do you want a cup of tea or coffee?"

"That would be great. Tea please."

She turned the kettle on. "Just help yourself to whatever you want in here at any time, Dan. There should be some Branston Pickle in the fridge if you want that on your sandwich. Sorry I wasn't around when you got back – I just went round to a friend's house for the evening."

"That's okay. I was surprised the house was open though."

"Oh it's pretty safe round here. We're open from about six o'clock in the morning during the summer because we start pretty early some days and then we finish when it gets dark sometimes too. So there's always someone about, either the lads who work here or groups coming back to get changed out of their wetsuits and have a shower. I normally just lock up when I go to bed. Anyway how was your day?"

"It was great fun. Ciaran treated me like one of his group so I got to do everything that they did. I was the guinea pig though. We went round the coast jumping off higher and higher rocks and I always had to go first, but that was okay. Until we got to that one that's like jumping off the roof of a house – Ciaran told me to keep my arms by my sides, but I put them out and they got smacked by the water as I landed. I won't do that again."

"I'm glad you enjoyed it," Bethan said as she put the mugs of tea on the table and sat down. Dan finished making his sandwich and sat down opposite her.

"We came back and the customers all got changed and headed off. And then Bez, Kermit and Donk came back and we went over to the pub. It was a great day – not like working at all."

"Well I gave Ciaran a ring just now on my way back and he said you did okay so it looks like you've passed your trial."

"Really? I didn't do anything apart from jump off rocks into the water and have fun. I wish all my probation days in my previous jobs had been as enjoyable as that."

"Ciaran said that you enjoyed yourself but more importantly that you were enthusiastic and encouraging with the customers. We want people to have a good time and the group leader sets the tone for that. It's not really something you can teach, but the main thing you need is enthusiasm. And of course it helps if you're a strong swimmer and aren't too clumsy when climbing up the rocks. Ciaran also said that you were very helpful with the youngsters and the more nervous people, guiding them up the rocks and encouraging them on the higher jumps."

"I just wanted to make sure that they were okay and had a good time."

"Well there you go," said Bethan. "You were obviously made to be an adventure sports leader." She finished her cup of tea and stood up. "Anyway in the morning just help yourself to cereal and toast – or whatever else you can find."

"What time do you want me to start in the morning?"

"We're starting a bit earlier tomorrow: about nine o'clock."

"Okay, I'll make sure I'm down in plenty of time."

"Right, I'm off to bed now," said Bethan, as she quickly washed out her mug and put it on the draining board. "I'm in the room next door to yours so I hope you don't snore too loudly."

Dan smiled, not knowing how to reply to this and acutely aware that they were the only two people in the house.

"Night, Dan," Bethan said briskly and headed out of the kitchen.

"Good night," said Dan, but she had already gone.

14. The Bitches. St Davids. Thursday Morning.

Bethan Geddes had been running kayaking and climbing sessions since she was fifteen years old. That's nearly twenty years, she thought to herself as she sat down at the desk in the office the next morning.

Her mother, Lorna, had been a keen kayaker since childhood and won a bronze medal for Scotland at the Commonwealth Games before deciding to travel the world. When she was twenty six, she met Hamish Geddes on a freezing cold river halfway down a mountain in Nepal when they were both invited to join a white water rafting trip organised by a mutual friend.

They were surprised to discover that they were both from villages around Glencoe in western Scotland and that they had grown up fifteen miles apart. Although Hamish was five years older they knew many of the same people from the Glencoe area.

From that moment they were inseparable and they travelled the world together for the next ten years before they decided to spend more time closer to home. They happened to spend some time kayaking around the Pembrokeshire coast and climbing the sea cliffs that overlooked the Atlantic Ocean – and they chose to stay, at least for a couple of years.

They worked in pubs and campsites to earn spending money so that they could indulge their pastimes but when Lorna was forty one – and Hamish forty six – she discovered to her delight that she was pregnant. They had already started to lay down roots in the area but this made them think about doing it properly.

During the first few years of Bethan's life, her parents worked hard to save enough money to buy a home. And then Lorna was left thirty thousand pounds by an aunt who had died and they were able to put down a deposit on a big old, run-down Victorian place called Alun House.

Hamish dedicated his weekends to renovating the building himself as best he could, both as a home and a base for the business that they were hoping to start. And then, when Bethan was ten years old, they launched Geddes Outdoor Sports.

Business was difficult at first, but then the trickle became a steady flow and, after a couple of years, took off to the point where they were able to take on two full-time instructors. Lorna was able to dedicate some time to spreading the word – she didn't like the term *marketing* – and Geddes Outdoor Sports earned them a good living for a number of years.

Bethan didn't think that her parents would ever have retired but when her mother was in her mid-sixties, she was diagnosed with motor neurone disease. Bethan had just returned from three years at university studying Business Studies and found herself taking on more and more of the work over the coming years as her father dedicated his time to looking after her mother.

Lorna Geddes lived a good life for another ten years with the support of her family, but her health deteriorated rapidly towards the end. Her father Hamish was by that point quite frail himself but did as much as he could for his wife.

When her mother died, Bethan herself was distraught but, after the activities around the funeral had finished, she saw that the light had gone out in her father's eyes. It was only four months later that her father passed away himself. One morning he didn't come down for breakfast and when she went upstairs she found him lying peacefully in his bed.

The doctor declared that he had died of heart failure, but her father's friends said that he had simply died of a broken heart.

In a way Bethan was pleased that her father was able to join her mother, but at the same time she felt abandoned. She was absurdly annoyed at her parents for having given birth to her at a relatively advanced age and for not giving her any siblings.

Bethan was tired. She needed a break from the stress of running Geddes Outdoor Sports. Money had been tight during the last few years of her parent's lives as they were unable to work and they had re-mortgaged Alun House. Every day she felt the pressure of having to pay her staff and satisfy the mortgage repayments.

Sometimes Bethan wished she had a normal office job, where she could simply work nine to five and know that the salary was going to arrive each month. But she knew she wouldn't be happy.

Stop feeling sorry for yourself and get on with your work, she thought to herself and paused as she thought she heard footsteps down the hallway – and at the same time heard the front door open.

She heard Dan and Bez wishing each other good morning in the hall and then both of them came into the office.

"Morning," said Bethan, glancing up for a moment, then fixing her eyes on the laptop again. "I'm pleased to say you didn't snore much last night, Dan," she said while she tapped away.

Bez glanced sharply from Dan to Bethan who was still concentrating on her work. He looked back at Dan and raised his eyebrows inquisitively.

Dan just smiled and shook his head.

Bethan pressed another key and sat back as the printer sprang into action.

"So, Dan," she said swivelling her chair to face him, "this morning we're going to introduce you to The Bitches."

"Right …" said Dan slowly, waiting for an explanation.

"Oh Dan," smiled Bez. "You won't like The Bitches. They bite new boys."

"Go on then, tell me who The Bitches are."

"Just off the coast to the west is a small island called Ramsey Island and the stretch of water between the mainland and the island is called Ramsey Sound," started Bethan. "When the tide comes in through the sound, it gets compressed by a combination of the rising sea bed and the land narrowing in on both sides. At certain times the sea can travel through Ramsey Sound at around twelve or thirteen miles an hour and waves can form that are sometimes five or six feet high. It's a great place for kayakers."

"Sounds good," said Dan, "but where do The Bitches come in?"

Bez couldn't resist chipping in: "The Bitches are some beauties in the narrowest part of the sound that make things even more fun. And their friends The Whelps. They're two sets of rocks in a line. As the tide floods into the sound the water goes up to cover the Bitches and Whelps and this creates a difference in water level of anywhere between one and four feet. The speed of the tide and the difference in the water height forms whirlpools, some great squirrely eddy lines, stoppers and, most importantly, big wave trains. It's some of the best playboating in Europe, man, which is pretty much why I live in St Davids." He paused for breath and then remembered: "And then there's Horse Rock."

"What's Horse Rock?" asked Dan.

"It's a pinnacle that sticks up from the sea floor in the middle of the sound a bit further up and creates a vicious set of whirlpools that can suck a paddler underwater if they're not careful."

"And you want me to help you take a group through all that?" said Dan. "I'm not sure if I'm the right person for the job."

Bez laughed. "Don't worry, man, you're just driving the Land Rover."

"Thank goodness for that," sighed Dan.

"Ciaran'll be out on the water with me. We just like to have someone on land keeping an eye out, just in case."

"Just in case what?"

"Anything. If someone gets hurt you're ready to take them off to hospital straight away; also you can look out for the weather and help people carrying their kayaks when they come out exhausted. It's just useful to have someone else around."

"I presume they're all experienced kayakers?" Dan asked.

"Yeah, me and Ciaran trained some of them up. The other people have been doing it for years, but haven't kayaked round here before and just want someone who knows the waters to guide them."

"Right, that's enough talking," said Bethan. "Can you two get the minibus loaded up, please. You've got to get the kayaks on the trailer and sort out the helmets, buoyancy aids and everything else. Show him what to do Bez."

"Let's go, Dan." Bez took the sheets that had just been printed and led Dan out to a minibus that was parked around the side of the house.

Bez put his printouts on the dashboard and then they pulled the trailer over and hooked it up to the minibus. Together they lifted kayaks out of a large shed, hauled them over with one person at each end and lifted them onto the racks of the trailer. They then loaded all the other equipment into the minibus.

While Bez checked the sheets again, Dan leaned against the front of the vehicle to rest. As he stood there, a car pulled in through the gates and started making its way down the driveway.

"Looks like one of our customers is arriving," Dan said and then he wondered why the four-wheel drive BMW seemed familiar.

"Nope," said Bez as he looked up. "That's trouble arriving."

Then Dan saw the number plate: R4YS J and his heart sank. It was the road rage man from a couple of days ago. What was he doing here in St Davids?

"I know him," said Dan. "I had an argument with him a couple of days ago. Or rather he had an argument with me."

"I'm not surprised," said Bez. "That's Rhys Jones. Runs a couple of businesses round here and thinks he owns the town. Well, he thinks he owns the whole of Wales actually."

"What's he doing here?"

"No idea. Let's pull the bus round to the front so it's ready for when the customers get here – and then see if Bethan needs any help dealing with him."

Bez jumped into the driver's seat and started the engine. Dan was about to walk round to the front of the house when he noticed that the front tyre was flat.

"Hang on, Bez," he shouted and pointed at the wheel. "You've got a flat tyre."

Bez got out again and looked at the tyre. He bent down to look at it more closely.

"Bloody hell," he said, running his finger along the hole. "I think it's been cut with a knife."

Dan knelt down and examined the wheel. "I think you're right," he said.

"We'd better get it changed quick. Actually I'll just check the others – I hope they're haven't been slashed as well." He walked round the front of the bus and looked at the tyres on the other side.

"Oh no," he said kicking the other front tyre. "This one's been done as well. The back ones seem okay though."

"I'm surprised we didn't notice them before," said Dan, shaking his head.

"We were busy with all the stuff I suppose."

"What are we going to do? You've only got one spare, haven't you?"

"Yeah." Bez kicked the tyre again. "Hang on, there's another minibus round the back of the shed. Kermit and Donk were going to use that for a climbing session this afternoon, but we'll take their spare and I'll get one of them to run over this morning to get the two tyres replaced."

Bez and Dan were just about to start the process of replacing the two tyres when they heard shouting from the front of the house.

"Sounds like Bethan," said Bez and they both set off at a run.

As they came around the corner, Rhys Jones was marching out of the front door with Bethan close behind him.

"Get out Rhys," she shouted at him. "And don't ever set foot in Alun House again or I'll call the police."

Jones turned around and laughed. "That's not much of a threat, Bethan. We both know the police round here – we went to school with most of them."

"Need any help, Bethan?" asked Bez, stepping forward.

On seeing the young man approach, Jones stepped back towards his car, and said "Don't touch me, lad. I'll sue you for assault." Then he noticed Dan just behind him. "Hey, I know you, don't I?" He looked at Dan more closely. "You were that idiot in Tenby the other day."

Dan was disappointed that the man had recognised him but said nothing.

"Bethan asked you to leave," said Bez marching forward another step but this time Jones didn't give any ground. The two men were face to face and looking threateningly at each other.

"Get away from me lad or I'll – "

"What will you do, old man?" shouted Bez. "And what do you know about the two tyres that have been slashed on our minibus?"

"What?" blurted Bethan, looking at Bez and then turning to Jones. "What have you done, Rhys?"

"Don't blame me for your own blunders," snarled Jones. "I've only just got here."

"Get out, Rhys."

"Don't worry, I'm going, Bethan, but you'll be begging me to come back soon when you've got no customers."

"Just go before I make you," said Bez.

The man got into his car and drove out with his wheels spinning, flicking stones up from the gravel driveway. The BMW disappeared out of the gate and they all breathed a sigh of relief.

"What was that all about?" said Bez as he turned to Bethan.

"I don't want to talk about it, Bez," she said, still angry from the encounter. "I'll tell you later. More importantly, what was that about tyres being slashed?"

"The two front tyres on the minibus are flat. They look like they've been cut. And then suddenly there's Rhys Jones. Coincidence?"

"I don't know," she replied, shaking her head. "Bez, can you take the wheels over to Haverfordwest to get the tyres replaced? You'll have to go as quick as you can."

"We don't need to Bethan. We were just about to put the spare on and we've also got the spare from the other minibus. And I'll ask Kermit to get them both sorted before his climbing group this afternoon. Is that okay?"

"That's a good idea, but we'll have to hope that you don't get another flat tyre. You'd better get cracking then. People should be arriving in a minute."

Bez and Dan walked quickly back round to the minibus and replaced the two wheels as swiftly as they could. Unfortunately the trailer had to be un-hitched during the wheel change and then re-hitched afterwards but they finished the job in around twenty minutes.

Dan jumped in the front passenger seat and Bez drove the bus round to the front of the house where half a dozen people were waiting with Bethan. She had made them mugs of tea and was chatting to them about the day ahead.

"Sorry for the slight delay, guys," said Bez as he pulled up and jumped out of the driver's door. "Have we got everyone who's meeting us here, Bethan?" After getting a nod from Bethan, he continued. "My name's Bez and this is Dan. We're picking up another instructor called Ciaran on the way and the three of us will be looking after you today. We're meeting some other customers over by Ramsey Sound and then I'll explain to everybody what we're doing today. It should be great fun. Okay, everybody climb aboard."

He pulled open the sliding door on the side of the minibus and the six people clambered in.

"Good luck, boys," said Bethan as Dan and Bez got into the front of the vehicle. "Don't worry about Kermit – I'll give him a call. You just concentrate on giving the customers a good time."

"We sure will," said Bez with a smile. "The Bitches will welcome them with open arms!"

He put the minibus into gear and set off. They went up the drive and turned onto the road.

The customers in the back were all chatting amongst themselves and Dan took the opportunity of talking quietly to Bez about what had happened that morning.

"What do you think that Rhys Jones bloke wanted then?" asked Dan.

"I've got no idea," shrugged Bez.

Dan shook his head, still not quite believing it. "You said he runs a couple of businesses locally – what sort of thing does he do?"

"It's all property related. His main business is an estate agents that has half a dozen offices round the area, but he also has holiday cottages that he rents out and he owns a few pubs, here and in Tenby."

"That's where I ran into him, in Tenby, when I was on my bike early in the morning. A weird road rage incident. Admittedly it was my fault but then he pulled across the road in front of me and started shouting at me."

"He shouts at everyone," said Bez, shaking his head. "It's his way of communicating. Anyway, there's Ciaran."

Dan noticed that they were now in the centre of the small town. They pulled over and Ciaran got into the double front passenger seat alongside Dan.

"Top of the morning, boys," said Ciaran. "What took you?"

Bez brought Ciaran up to date with all that had happened including the flat tyres and the heated exchange with Rhys Jones.

"And another thing," said Bez, smiling at Dan. "I was in the office with Bethan this morning and then Dan saunters in and Bethan says to him 'you didn't snore much last night'! What do you think of that?"

"You don't hang around, do you Dan?" laughed Ciaran, nudging him.

"It's nothing like that boys," Dan replied. "It's just that I'm in the room next door to hers and -"

"And you sneaked through in the middle of the night," laughed Bez.

"You just wish it had been you, Bezzy," said Ciaran.

"You bet I do," he nodded. "By the way, Kate and I aren't speaking again."

"Again?" said Ciaran. "What is it this time?" He turned to Dan. "Don't worry. They've been together for years and Bez'll never leave her. He's too scared and she likes having someone she can boss around I reckon. Anyway Bez what did you do this time?"

"Last year I got this ski-walker exercise machine. I've probably only used it about a dozen times and it's just been sitting there in the middle of the lounge since then. Well I got home last night and decided to put it in the garage. Kate told me not to though. She said wait until her Dad comes over at the weekend, but I told her I didn't need anyone's help. So I dragged it out into the hall and then somehow one end of it got hooked under the radiator."

"Oh no, I can guess what you're going to say," said Ciaran, grimacing.

"Well it was kind of stuck and I twisted it and turned it, but I couldn't go forwards and I couldn't even go back again. Kate said I should have waited until her Dad came over and that wound me up so I pulled it really hard and the radiator just flipped off. I couldn't believe it."

"Typical Bez," Ciaran could hardly speak he was laughing so hard.

"It just flipped off?" said Dan, horrified. "What did you do?"

"Water was pouring out of the two pipes that stick up out of the floor so I put my thumbs over them both. I was sitting there in between the ski-walker and the radiator on the wet carpet and I couldn't let go. And Kate was stood there telling me that I should have waited for her Dad. I shouted at her to turn the water off, but neither of us knew where the stopcock was and she couldn't find it. So she tried to phone a plumber but she couldn't get hold of anyone at that time of night, so in the end she phoned her Dad and he came over. He turned everything off and put the radiator back on and Kate thought he was brilliant."

Ciaran's laughter had ratcheted up as Bez had explained each new step of the story and by this point the customers in the back of the minibus were listening in. Unfortunately they had missed the start of the story so Bez had to go through it all again.

"And the worst thing was," said Bez, "Kate's Dad put the bloody ski-walker back in the lounge because he needed to clear some space to put the radiator back on."

"Brilliant," laughed Ciaran. "It could only happen to you, Bez."

"And Kate gave me the silent treatment for the rest of the night and didn't say a word to me this morning. But it's ridiculous – it wasn't my fault. So I'm not going to crack first."

"This is normal, Dan," said Ciaran. "At least once a month they have an argument where they don't speak for a few days."

Ciaran and Bez continued chatting as they drove over towards Ramsey Sound. Dan looked out of the window at the cathedral and the ruined Bishops Palace as they left St Davids heading west towards the interestingly named St Justinians.

The terrain on the way to the coast was curious and unusual. He saw three low gnarly hills – rocky outcrops that rose like mini volcanos out of the otherwise flat landscape. They travelled past areas of countryside that were damp and swampy with large fields of bull rushes and reeds that looked like white bamboo.

They drove up a tarmac road that felt more like a track and about ten minutes after leaving St Davids they pulled to a stop in a small parking area. Dan got out of the bus and looked around. They were high above the sea and a few hundred yards across the water he saw a long grass-covered island edged by tall cliffs. He presumed this was Ramsey Island. Some winding steps lead down from the small car park to a lifeboat station at the water's edge. A man was just coming to the top of the steps.

Ciaran waved to the man as Bez parked the minibus. "Hey, Bez, it's Geraint," said Ciaran. "Can you do the talk to the customers and I'll introduce Dan to the old man."

Ciaran led Dan over to where the man was waiting by his car as they approached. Dan thought the man was not so old – he estimated him to be in his early forties, with a few streaks of grey in his hair. He was short and stocky with rugged features.

"Hi, Geraint," said Ciaran, shaking his hand. "How are you?"

"Fine. You?" Geraint's economy of speech made Dan smile.

"Great. We're just taking some people down the sound. It's a nice day for it." Ciaran looked up at the blue skies above them to confirm his statement.

"Uh-huh," agreed Geraint.

"I thought I'd introduce you to Dan – he's just started working with us." Dan held out his hand and almost flinched at Geraint's bear-like grip. Ciaran turned to Dan. "Geraint is one of the four coxswains at the lifeboat station here. Well his day job is farming but he seems to be here more than he's on his farm. Have we still got a drill this weekend, Geraint?"

"Uh-huh. Don't let me down, boy."

"I'll be there, sir," said Ciaran deferentially.

"Are you in the lifeboat crew then?" asked Dan, a little surprised.

"Yeah and Bez. Bethan made it a condition of the job, but I'm really glad she did. It's really worthwhile even if sometimes when you're out there in a big storm you start wondering why you ever volunteered, eh Geraint?"

"Uh-huh," Geraint grunted. Looking at his expression, Dan didn't think the man would be worried by anything. He hoped that if he ever needed to be rescued at sea, then someone like Geraint would be in charge.

"How often are you called out?" asked Dan.

"Sometimes a month or two will go by without a shout – and then you'll get three shouts in a week."

"And it's all run by volunteers, isn't it? It's amazing that people give up their time, especially in this day and age."

"Yeah, there's about twenty-five of us who take it in turns to be on call and the boat takes a crew of six. You get the shout and you come running, then we all jump in the boat and it slides down that ramp there."

Dan turned to look down at the lifeboat station properly for the first time and he saw that the building was twenty or thirty feet above the water. A wood, concrete and steel framework supported a hundred metre slipway that ran down into the water. He thought it looked like part of a roller-coaster or a log flume.

"That looks fun," he said.

"Yeah, it's great when you're on a drill in nice weather, but in the dark with thunder and lightning all around you it's a different kettle of fish."

"See you Sat'day," Geraint said suddenly and, without waiting for a reply, got into his four-wheel drive Nissan truck and drove off.

"Let's go and sort out the kayaks before Bez moans at us," said Ciaran.

The two of them started unloading the kayaks from the back of the trailer while Bez finished explaining the plan for the day to the group.

Dan then helped people carrying the kayaks down the steps to the slipway beside the lifeboat station and generally assisted with whatever was required to get the group onto the water. All of the people were experienced kayakers and it wasn't long before the whole group was bobbing in front of Bez and Ciaran as they gave their final instructions.

"We've got an hour or so before it starts getting exciting out there," said Ciaran to the group in front of him. "So we'll paddle through the route and we'll show you where the safe havens are in case you get into trouble. And the places to avoid of course. Then we'll dive in and have some fun. Follow me."

Ciaran turned to paddle out across the sound and Bez waited to take up the rear.

Dan shielded his eyes against the morning sun and looked out across the water. Ramsey Island looked like it was lying on top of the sea around 800 yards away from where he was standing. The island was flat for most of its two mile length, but was punctuated by two hills dividing it into thirds. He could just make out some buildings at the base of each hill and from the strong breeze on his face he assumed that they were facing the mainland to hide from the prevailing winds coming in from the Atlantic.

At the southern end of the island was a jumble of smaller hills and mounds – along with a cluster of smaller islands.

Ramsey Island's flat surface was around a hundred metres above the level of the sea and for the most part the land that fell away to the water was steep but grass-covered. However at various places the sea had gnawed away at the island's edges to form inlets and firths.

About halfway down the island he could see the Bitches and the Whelps at a point where the sound narrowed to around 400 yards across. The line of rocks stretched from the island a hundred yards into the sound and at present they were still above the level of the water.

Dan was looking forward to watching the kayakers navigating Ramsey Sound on this lovely sunny spring morning. He sat down on some rocks to enjoy the show.

15. Graded Grains Make Finer Sand. Tenby.
Thursday Midday.

Jess arrived on the same early morning train with which Andrew had travelled to Tenby the day before. She came out of the station and saw Andrew waiting in his hire car. Putting her bag in the back, she got into the front passenger seat.

"Hi Andy. Thanks for picking me up, pet," she said and patted his leg.

Andrew gave a slight jump at the contact, but decided to ignore it. His name was another matter though. "Hello Jessica, but can I say something? I prefer to be called Andrew actually. Andy seems like a young person's name."

"You seem like quite a young person to me, Andy. Anyway we should get to work, shouldn't we?"

Andrew put the car into gear and set off. He didn't quite know what to say, or rather he wanted to say many things all at the same time: you think I seem like a young person? You called me Andy again and I still prefer Andrew. I'm the boss here, don't tell me that we should get to work. Why did you pat me on the leg?

"Where are we off to then?" Jess said, puncturing the silence created by Andrew's competing thoughts.

"Well," he sighed, "I worked through some little places called Penally, Jameston and Skrinkle Haven this morning but nobody had seen our man. The next place along the coast is Manorbier."

"Oh yes, Manorbier is a nice place. It's only a small village, but there's a nice pub and a big ruined castle. And a lovely beach at low tide."

Andrew was surprised at her recognition of the place but then remembered. "Did you say you went to university here?"

"Yes, at Swansea. I studied Marine Biology and we covered the whole of the South Wales coast. In fact my final year project was a study of the varying sizes of the grains of sand on the beaches along this coast."

"I'm not sure if that sounds boring or interesting," Andrew said.

"It was quite interesting actually – did you know that the sand round here is quite fine-grained and the sand on the other side of the Severn estuary on the Devon coast is much more coarse-grained?"

"Why did you study Marine Biology? It seems a strange subject for someone who joined the police."

"Did you know," said Jess, smiling at him, "that these are the first personal questions you've asked about me in the three weeks that we've worked together? Why is that?"

Andrew thought for a moment. "I suppose I wasn't really interested in knowing anything about you," he shrugged.

"Ha. You don't mince your words, do you, Andy?" She laughed. "Has there been a change of heart now then? You're interested in knowing more about me now, perhaps?"

"Not at all," he said quickly. "I only asked why you had studied round here because I felt that your knowledge of the area might come in handy."

"Hmmm maybe," she said. "I think that the reason you didn't talk to me at first was because you felt threatened by my arrival at DHC and now that we're out in the field, where you feel at ease, you're happier to chat."

Once again, many thoughts whirled around Andrew's head competing to get out first. "I'm not sure if I feel at ease now," he muttered, more to himself than Jess.

"You shouldn't have felt threatened by my arrival though," she said.

"I wasn't," he insisted.

"Because I know I will never be as good as you at the investigative side of the business. When we were writing up the procedures for the new team, you made points that I would never have considered. Often they were obvious when you'd explained them, but for you it's instinctive to know how an investigator or his subject are thinking."

"I've never really thought about it."

"Like I said, it's instinct for you," she said. "But can't you see that I know more about the business process side of things than you? And if we work together we can make a success of the Personal Injury Claim Unit?"

"I'm not really interested in the Personal Injury Claim Unit," Andrew shrugged.

"I know. Richard told me and he said that I would have to coax the information out of you and he was right. Why aren't you interested in it though?"

"I don't want to follow someone who's claiming they've hurt their back just to see if they're playing badminton or going dancing."

"But do you think that it's right that someone is claiming thousands of pounds for an injury they don't have?"

"Absolutely not. It's a form of thieving and it makes everyone's insurance premiums go up. I don't see why everybody should suffer just because a few people –"

"Exactly!" interrupted Jess. "Now you're starting to get passionate about it. So we agree the objectives of the new unit are worthwhile and also it will make money for DHC and save money for the insurance companies. And the false claimants will get prosecuted. So let's make the Personal Injury Claim Unit as good as it can be. I'll do all the donkey work, but you tell me the best way to run it."

"Mmmm," he murmured non-committally.

She looked at him. "And you won't have to do the surveillance yourself. You know that don't you?"

"Yes, of course I do," he mumbled grudgingly like a sullen teenager.

"And another thing."

Andrew glanced over at her. "Yes," he said, wondering what was coming next.

"You didn't exactly make me feel welcome when I joined the company. I was nervous on my first day, you know."

"You didn't seem like it."

"Luckily Richard told me that you were a miserable old bugger." She patted him on the knee again and smiled at him. Andrew almost swerved into a car coming the other way. "So the next time you start working with someone," she continued, "perhaps you could take their feelings into account."

"I'm not interested in their feelings."

"I know you're not. Don't you think that's funny though? That you're so instinctive about how a criminal is feeling, but you have no insight into your colleagues' feelings."

"I've never really thought about that," said Andrew.

"Don't worry," Jess said. "I'll get you trained up. It may take a few years though." She laughed and Andrew just concentrated on the road.

"Anyway," she continued, "what's the plan today? After Manorbier I mean."

"We'll just work further along the coast," replied Andrew. "There are some other places called Bosherton, Stackpole and Freshwater East. They're all small places, but there are quite a few caravan parks, holiday villages as well as odd pubs here and there. The last place along the coast this side of Milford Haven is Angle. We might get there by the end of the day. Do you know Angle?"

"Yes, but why are we going there?"

"The same reason as we're going to all these places. Because they're west of Tenby and I think he's heading that way."

"What makes you think he's going in that direction?" she asked.

"I told you on the phone yesterday. He was in Saundersfoot ten days ago working at a pub called The Captains Table."

"Oh yes, I've been there." She thought for a moment. "Or have I? Is that the one by the harbour?"

"Yes," he sighed.

"Then I have been there. I had a pint of Guiness and we sat and watched the boats coming and going. It was a lovely sunny evening. So why are we going to Angle?"

"I thought you knew this area. Are you being deliberately obtuse?"

"There's no need to be like that about it."

Andrew calmed himself down and explained slowly: "He was in Saundersfoot ten days ago. He was in Tenby yesterday. That means he must be going west."

"Oh yes," she said quickly. "I got Saundersfoot and Tenby the wrong way round. I thought Tenby was furthest west out of the two of them."

"It is!" Andrew said in raised voice and then tried to speak calmly. "Well the coast dips down at that point and Tenby is actually south-west of Saundersfoot." He glanced at Jess's perplexed face. "Oh forget it, just trust me." He shook his head and glanced over at the ocean as he drove along the winding country road. "It's going to be a long day," he sighed.

-o-o-o-

That evening they checked into The Hibernia Inn in the village of Angle on the very end of a peninsula that formed the bottom jawbone of the huge mouth of Milford Haven. This extensive estuary was once declared the finest natural deep-water harbour in the world by Admiral Nelson.

They had spent the day looking for a trace of Cullen along the stunning Pembrokeshire coast without success. It was seven o'clock when they tried The Hibernia Inn – with another negative outcome – and Andrew had decided it would be a good place to spend the night. The old pub, named for one of the four ships of the Royal Navy which from 1765 to 1921 bore the name of HMS Hibernia, was just his cup of tea. They had agreed to meet in the bar for a bite to eat after taking their bags to their rooms and getting changed.

"You know that last beach we stopped at this afternoon?" asked Jess, as they sat in the bar waiting for their food. "Freshwater West it was called."

"The ones with the sand dunes?"

"Yes, that's right," she nodded. "That's my favourite beach along this coast. Those huge sand dunes covered with long grass. And the colours are strange as the land stretches away up to the hills: it's like a rolling green carpet flecked with millions of cream green cotton wool balls. And the sand itself, especially the sand that had blown across the road, it's an unusual orange colour … I know, it's a kind of paprika orange."

"You've got a vivid imagination," remarked Andrew.

"Didn't you see it?"

"Well I saw the sand but it just looked like sand to me."

Jess made a dismissive harrumphing noise, but fortunately for Andrew the landlady arrived with their food at that moment.

"There you go," she said, putting their plates down on the table. "They're home-made chips of course and I made you a few extra."

Andrew stared at the huge portion of chips on his plate. "Thank you," he said. "They look lovely. I'm not sure if I'll manage them all though."

"Don't let me down now," smiled the landlady and headed back to the kitchen.

"Thanks for giving Iceland a nudge the other day, by the way," said Andrew, spearing a chip with his fork.

"It's a pleasure," smiled Jess appreciatively. "It's kind of you to mention it. You must be starting to worry about my feelings."

Andrew ignored her comment. "Vinod told me yesterday evening that they sent a load of data over and he and Nigel were ploughing through it. I'm going to give Vinod a ring later and see if they've made any progress with it. How did you get them to get their act together?"

"I may not be very good at my east and west – or left and right for that matter – but I'm good with people. And I don't give up. I had to speak to about a dozen people and imply a dozen threats but I finally got to someone who was high enough up the chain of command. He said he'd just returned from holiday so I simply made sure that our request was the first thing he looked at."

"By the way, you never answered my question earlier."

"What question was that?" Jess replied.

"Why did you come down here to study Marine Biology and then go back to join the police in Newcastle?"

"Aha, so you are interested in me," she smiled and Andrew looked down quickly and shuffled his food on his plate.

"Well," Jess replied after a second, "I'd spent a few years training to do athletics and then got a bad injury which ended any hopes I'd had of making a career of it. After a few months of moping around I decided to go to university and I just liked the sound of the Marine Biology course. Simple as that really. I suppose I also wanted to see a bit of the country outside of the north-east and Swansea was a great place to go."

"Which athletics discipline did you do?"

"Eight hundred metres," she said and added proudly: "I came third in the national junior championships when I was seventeen."

"That's impressive," nodded Andrew. "And I was about to say that I did a bit of running at school. How did you get injured?"

"I tore my anterior cruciate ligament in a school hockey match."

Andrew raised his eyebrows. "I've heard about footballers whose careers were ended by an ACL injuries but that was twenty years ago. I thought things had got a bit better these days."

"In football if you lose a few per cent of your speed people might not notice it, but in athletics a few percent means you finish last."

Andrew nodded thoughtfully. "So why did you join the police?"

"What else would you do after studying Marine Biology?" Jess joked. "I looked for jobs in that field but there aren't too many marine biologist positions going each year. I went back home to Newcastle to live with my parents while I looked for a proper job and was doing some temping in the meantime. I got a job for a couple of months doing admin for the Northumbria Police and when that finished a full time job came up. My boss suggested I apply for it and I got it. And I've never looked back." She smiled.

Andrew nodded and took another mouthful of his huge portion of beer-battered cod and chips. He looked around at the naval memorabilia that adorned the walls and ceiling of the pub. He studied the photographs of HMS Invincible, HMS Illustrious and dozens of other aircraft carriers and ships that were on the wall around their table.

Jess studied him as he took a long drink of his pint of bitter and licked his lips.

"Here's a question for you," she said. "If society collapsed would you rather go without tea or beer?"

Andrew opened his mouth to say beer and then closed it again. He did like a nice cup of tea.

"I decline to answer," he said in the end. "On the basis that it's not going to happen."

She laughed. "If you don't answer then you lose."

"I don't accept that premise. If I don't answer then it's as if the question never existed."

"It's just a game," she smiled.

"That's the sort of game Vinod likes – you should play with him. He asked me all sorts of stupid questions like what superpower would I want if I was a superhero."

"That's easy," Jess said. "The power to change into any animal. Then you could be really fast like a cheetah or fly like a bird or be really strong like a gorilla or – "

"It's a stupid game," he interrupted. "And you're cheating by having multiple powers."

"You're almost playing by saying that," she contended. Andrew nearly argued again but decided his silence might be a stronger deterrent to the continuation of the game. He concentrated his attention on his meal.

"It was tiring today," Jess said after a while. "Going into all those places and asking the same question over and over again."

"Aye, I suppose so," Andrew nodded and sipped his pint again.

"You don't seem down-hearted that nobody recognised him. And we went into a lot of places."

"I suppose you've just got to be patient in this business. Methodical."

"Leave no stone un-turned?"

"Aye," he nodded and then glanced up at her when he realised that she was making fun of him.

"Tell me about Cullen," she said, still smiling at him. "What sort of person is he?"

"You've read the reports."

"But you've actually met him. Tell me about his character."

Andrew thought for a moment. "He's a friendly person when you get talking to him, but happy to be alone as well. He's quite bright, not just book-smart but also has a lot of common sense. I've thought about his approach to being on the run and I can't think of anything better. He travels by bike and stays in a tent so he doesn't have any financial needs, apart from food, and he spends the minimum amount of time in each place. Any longer and you start to lay down roots or people starting wanting to know more about you. Any shorter and you wouldn't be able to get a job so you couldn't pay for your food."

"But if he stole all that money then why does he need to work?"

"He sounded quite principled. The money that he stole all went to his niece for her medical expenses and I believed him when he said he didn't use any of it for himself."

"I thought that was the first million? He's got another nine million in his back pocket, hasn't he?"

"True, but my guess is that he's got some reason for stealing the rest of the money. There must be if he's working in these places. And he struck me as the sort of person who would be doing it for a reason that was important to him."

"You sound as if you like him?"

"I said he was principled but I don't agree with his principles. I don't believe that it's right to steal."

"So where do you think we might find him?"

"He could be anywhere. If he's any good then he'll be where we least expect him to be. He could easily be in another part of the country and we're just wasting our time here."

"You must think about it at times. What would be your best bet for the kind of place that he might be?"

"There's no point. We've got to be methodical about it."

"Just pretend it's a game for a minute."

"Another game?"

"Humour me," she smiled. "Think of it as educating me if that helps."

Andrew nodded acceptance and considered the options. "Well as I said, he could be anywhere, but he's athletic and he likes water and the sea. Of course that's one of the reasons he's working along the coast – as well as that being where most of the tourism areas are. But I was thinking that his preferred job would be on the water or something sporty."

"So why don't we look at those kinds of places first?"

"Because Cullen can't afford to pick and choose. He gets to a new place and just tries to get a job anywhere that will have him."

"Okay," she nodded. "What about geographical location?"

"You want somewhere remote but not too remote. Otherwise you stand out too much. You want a small town or large village where it's commonplace for new people to turn up for a few days. These touristy parts of the country are perfect."

"What's the most likely place round here?" Jess asked.

"Tenby was pretty good. The places we tried this afternoon are perhaps too small really. Somewhere like Haverfordwest, St Davids, Pembroke Dock or Fishguard would be the right sort of size."

"Out of those, which one would you choose?"

"St Davids I think. The others are primarily working towns or ports and St Davids is a more likely place for tourists to turn up."

"So why don't we go and look for him there tomorrow?"

"You can't just flit about where you *think* he might be. It's a methodical process of elimination otherwise you might miss the place where he's actually hiding."

"I remember St Davids," said Jess thoughtfully. "It's a nice little town."

Andrew was interested in her knowledge of the town. "What do you think then? Did it seem a good place for Cullen to base himself for a few days?"

"I think so. I don't know really. I can't imagine what I would do if I was on the run. Go to a friend's place I suppose."

"Too easy. I looked into all of his friends at an early stage. Well, I won't know if I covered them all but we monitored the houses of his main friends for a while. And we're still keeping an eye on them along with his family." Andrew took another sip of his beer. "Anyway it's useful that you know this area from your time at university."

"We only covered the stretch up to here on my degree, but I stayed the night in St Davids when I walked the Pembrokeshire Coastal Path with my boyfriend."

"Your boyfriend?" For some reason, Andrew felt slightly deflated at the mention of Jess having a boyfriend.

"Well, he was my boyfriend at the time, but we got married a few months later."

"Oh right," said Andrew. He looked out of the window for a few seconds not knowing what to say. He now remembered Jess mentioning that she was married in her first few days at DHC. He felt foolish and abruptly he stood up. "Right I'm going up to my room to give Vinod a call. Can I suggest we meet down here for breakfast at seven thirty?"

"Okay …" Jess started saying, but Andrew had already turned and was walking away. I thought we were having a nice chat but he really is a miserable old bugger, she thought to herself.

-o-o-o-

Andrew sat on the end of the bed in his hotel room and wondered at his faint feeling of melancholy. He shook his head, frustrated with himself, and dialled Vinod's number.

"Hi Andy," said Vinod when he answered.

Andrew could hear the smile in the younger man's voice and he scowled. "I'm not in the mood, Vinod."

"Sorry Andrew," Vinod said quickly.

"I've phoned for an update on what you've found out today."

"Well, you remember that yesterday we worked out that the money in Iceland looked like it had come back to half a dozen ZBS accounts in the UK?"

"Of course."

"Well this morning we worked out which accounts they were. And they were indeed for half a dozen ZBS accounts for people at addresses in London. Daniel Akane, Daniel Anderson, Daniel Mantech, Daniel Pittendreigh, Daniel More, and Daniel Garioch."

"They're all called Daniel?" said Andrew in surprise.

"Yes, but guess what?"

"What?"

"They don't exist. Well there are people with those names obviously and we even found a couple that had the same date of birth, but none of them lived at the address that was given. Nigel thinks that they're made-up names."

Andrew was ahead of him. "So they're accounts set up by Cullen?"

"We think so," Vinod said. "He must like the name Dan."

"He said something about that in Cornwall. Another weakness which hopefully we should be able to exploit," Andrew said. "Is the money in these accounts then? Or has it been moved on again?"

"Well each account had about a million and a half in it, but they've all now got exactly one pound in them."

"Okay, so where does the money go next?"

"We haven't got that far yet. We were making sure that all the incoming payments matched up in case some money was going somewhere else."

"But the accounts have multiple withdrawals?"

"Oh yes, lots of different outgoing transactions. Hundreds of them in each account and some of them seem to go to the same place, but we're going to try and get to the bottom of it tomorrow."

"Is that it then?"

"Yes," Vinod said, slightly defensively. "There's a lot of data to wade through and that's as far as we've got for now. We spent most of the day trying to work out who these people were."

"Okay I'll talk to you tomorrow."

"Er, Andrew?"

"Yes?"

"Are you thinking of phoning for an update each day?"

"Until you've got to the bottom of it."

"May I ask why don't you phone Nigel?"

"He answers my questions with numbers. A lot of them. And I want words. You appreciate what the numbers mean."

"Oh right," said Vinod. "I'm pleased I'm doing something right."

"Don't let it go to your head."

"Well, um, is there any chance that you could, er, phone me in office hours next time."

"Why?" Andrew didn't understand why Vinod should say such a thing.

"Well you know, I kind of like having my evenings off."

Andrew laughed loudly. Vinod wasn't sure if he had heard him laugh before – it sounded somewhat disconcerting. "What you need to remember, young man," Andrew said in the schoolteacher's voice that Vinod had heard before, "is that our office hours are twenty four hours a day. The admin people might work nine to five, but you and I follow people in the evening and through the night. We never sleep."

"Yes, but that's just what it says on our website. We do sleep really. We have to."

"It's not just a slogan on a web page – it's our company ethos."

"I understand it's our ethos, but –"

"Vinod?"

"Yes, Andrew?"

"You're arguing too much now," he said. "By the way, *you* could phone *me* you know. Like I asked you to yesterday."

"Oh, okay. I'll do that then. I'll call you at the end of the afternoon tomorrow and give you an update."

"Perfect. And if I don't answer it's because I'm busy so you'll need to call back later. Don't just leave a message."

"Yes, but –"

"Goodbye, Vinod."

Vinod admitted defeat. "Goodbye, Andrew," he said.

16. The Bishops. St Davids. Thursday Late Evening.

Just after eight o'clock that same evening, Dan came downstairs to the kitchen. He was surprised to hear the sound of someone in the office and he popped his head round the door.

"Hi Bethan," he said, seeing her sitting at the desk, her long reddish-brown hair tied back in a ponytail. She was working at the computer and glanced over at him.

"Oh hello, Dan," she said, sitting back and stretching. He watched her long limbs unfurl sensuously like a cat stretching in front of the fire. "I'm just printing the sheets for tomorrow so I don't have to get up so early in the morning."

"I was going to have a cup of tea if that's okay?" he asked.

"Of course it is, Dan. I've told you, just help yourself to whatever's in the kitchen."

"Would you like a cup of tea or something?"

"No thanks," she said. "As soon as I've finished this I'm going down to the pub. Hey, do you want to come along?"

"Er …" Dan wasn't sure what to answer. What was she suggesting exactly?

Bethan didn't seem to notice his confusion as she turned back to the computer to continue with her work. "Bez and Ciaran are normally down there on a Thursday as well," she said as she clicked on a few things and the printer started humming.

"That would be great actually," Dan said, understanding that she was simply suggesting a drink with his new work colleagues.

"Good," she said, picking up the printouts. "I'm nearly finished."

Dan waited while she completed her work, closed down the computer and switched off the office light.

"I wanted to ask you," Dan said as they left the house and started down the gravel drive. "What happened with Rhys Jones this morning? You didn't seem very happy with him."

"That's an understatement," she said. "A few months ago he offered to buy the house and he's been badgering me about it ever since. I've said no on multiple occasions, but he keeps coming back."

Dan was surprised. "He just offered to buy the house? Not the business?"

"That's right, just the house and the grounds. The trouble is, he won't take no for an answer. In fact this morning he started making veiled threats and that's what made me so angry."

"What do you mean? What sort of threats?"

"Nothing explicit, but we've had a couple of unfortunate incidents over the last few weeks and he said it would be a shame if somebody found out about them. He told me that I should sell the house to him now because if the Health and Safety Executive closed us down then he'd offer a lot less."

"What sort of incidents have you had?"

"Nothing too serious fortunately. A couple of minor injuries on one of our team building sessions and another time one of our kayaks fell off the back of the trailer. There was a car a little way behind and it managed to stop in plenty of time. Thank goodness."

"And then the tyres on the minibus were slashed this morning," Dan added. "And they were definitely cut with a knife, there's no way they were blowouts or punctures. Do you think the other incidents were caused deliberately?"

Bethan considered his question. "I didn't at the time," she mused, "but I suppose somebody could have tampered with the ties on the trailer or the equipment for the team building exercise. But Rhys wouldn't do that."

"Wouldn't he? He's not the most friendly person."

"He's okay. Just a bit competitive that's all."

"Why does he want to buy your house though?"

"I don't know. He just said that he's always liked it. But I'm not selling – it's the house I grew up in and I don't have anything else now that my parents have died."

Dan nodded and waited for Bethan to continue.

"Let's talk about something else," she said. "How was your day over at Ramsey Sound?"

"It was great," Dan said. "It's a stunning place and it was interesting watching the guys kayaking around there. Oh and we met a guy called Geraint at the lifeboat station there. I was surprised to hear that Bez and Ciaran work in the lifeboat crew."

"Oh yes," Bethan nodded enthusiastically. "I was in the crew for ten years and I was keen that they play their part in the community as well. They've grown up a bit since working on the lifeboat. It's taught them responsibility."

"I think they would be pretty good people to have in a lifeboat actually."

"Absolutely. They know the waters round here and they're young and strong. And you need to be brave to go out into a howling storm. Because they work and play on the water they know what they're getting into."

"I'm sure they're brave when they need to be," nodded Dan. "Having seen them kayaking in Ramsey Sound today in all that white water, I can't imagine anyone better for working on the lifeboats."

They continued chatting as they walked and after a few minutes they arrived at the stone cross that marked the centre of the city. Bethan led Dan over the central square to a pub called The Bishops and they went in and found Ciaran and Bez at the bar.

They joined their friends at the bar and got some drinks.

"Didn't Kate want to come tonight?" Bethan asked Bez.

"They're not talking again!" interrupted Ciaran, laughing.

"Again?" said Bethan. "What is it this time?"

"Oh nothing. I don't want to talk about it," Bez said sullenly. "Anyway I've got bad news for you – Rhys is here." He nodded his head towards the other end of the pub where Rhys Jones was sitting at a small table with another man. They were deep in conversation.

"Is that Hugh Gardiner with him?" asked Bethan, peering through the crowded bar.

"Yup," said Bez and had another sip of his drink.

"Who's Hugh Gardiner?" asked Dan.

"He runs one of the hotels," replied Ciaran, "and he's also on the city council."

Dan couldn't get used to the small place of St Davids being referred to as a city.

"I wonder what he's doing with Rhys?" Bethan said. "I don't remember them being friends. In fact I didn't think Hugh liked him particularly."

"Does anyone?" laughed Ciaran.

Bethan decided to ignore Rhys and turned back to face her friends.

"Dan said he enjoyed his day at Ramsey Sound," she said to Ciaran and Bez.

"We'll get you in a kayak next time, Dan," said Ciaran. "We could get you trained up in a few weeks."

"I was only planning to stay for a week or so actually."

"Just a week? Why don't you stay a bit longer. He can stay a few more weeks, can't he, Bethan?"

"I'd be happy to for him to stay – he's pretty cheap," joked Bethan. "Seriously, Dan, if you'd like to stay until the summer or even just a couple of weeks that would be fine by me. I might even consider paying you."

Dan didn't answer for a moment. He was tempted to remain in St Davids. Surely he would be safe here for a while? And he had stumbled onto an interesting job and some nice people. What would be the harm in staying for a few weeks?

"Can I have a think about it?" he replied eventually.

"That's fine," Bethan answered. "Just let me know in the next few days."

"What are we doing tomorrow then Bethan?" asked Ciaran.

"Kermit and Donk are going to run a team building day for a bunch of solicitors from Swansea. You're taking a group out on the boat looking at the seals."

"I like seals," said Ciaran turning to face Dan.

"Yeah?" Dan replied, slightly surprised that Ciaran had commented on the subject, but out of the corner of his eyes he noticed Bez holding his head in his hands.

"I couldn't eat a whole one though," Ciaran laughed and everyone else groaned. Dan shook his head.

"He's an idiot," said Bez. "What are Dan and I doing tomorrow then Beth?"

"You're taking a small group climbing at the sea cliff at Porthclais."

"Sea cliff?" asked Dan.

"Yes, it's a sixty foot cliff overlooking St Brides Bay. You start by abseiling down to some rocks just above the water line and then you climb back up."

"Sounds fun," Dan said, but thought it sounded scary.

"Bez will look after you," she smiled.

As they were speaking, Dan saw Rhys Jones and Hugh Gardiner stand up from their table at the far end of the bar and put their jackets on. They started walking towards the front door at their side of the pub. Bethan saw Dan looking past her and turned to see what had caught his interest. She was surprised to see Rhys Jones standing right in front of her, with Hugh Gardiner waiting patiently just behind.

"Have you thought any more about my offer, Bethan?" he said.

"Oh for God's sake, Rhys, you're like a broken record. The answer is no."

"You can move to another place and run the business from there. I'm just interested in the property."

"So you keep saying. Why are you so interested in my house, Rhys?"

Dan was surprised that Rhys Jones had started this discussion in the middle of a pub and he glanced around to see what other people were making of it. Some of the bystanders at the bar were listening surreptitiously and some were openly staring. Bez and Ciaran had been studiously concentrating on their pints, but he noticed Ciaran now getting agitated each time Jones spoke.

"I've got a few development ideas for it, that's all." Rhys Jones answered the question eventually. Hugh Gardiner stepped back as if to distance himself from the conversation.

"What sort of development ideas?" asked Bethan.

"That's confidential at this stage."

"Is it really, Rhys? Well I don't care anyway. It's my home and it's not for sale. Since my parents died this is all I have left. You should know that Rhys."

"Look, Bethan, - "

Ciaran could hold himself back no longer. "What is it about 'not for sale' that you don't understand Rhys?" he said in a loud voice, stepping forward and jabbing a finger in Jones' direction.

"This has got nothing to do with you, Colin," Jones said.

"My name is Ciaran, you – "

"It's okay, Ciaran," said Bethan, putting a hand on his arm. "I can handle Rhys myself."

Ciaran took a step back but Dan could tell that he was fuming.

Rhys Jones glanced at Ciaran dismissively and turned back to Bethan. "I should let you know that if there are any more incidents endangering the safety of the public it would be my moral duty to pass this on to the authorities."

"That would be the first time in your life that you've had any morals, Rhys," Bethan replied.

"Just think about my offer, Bethan. I'll call in and see you in a couple of days."

Rhys Jones turned and left the pub, with Hugh Gardiner following behind him.

Everyone in the bar seemed to sigh with relief.

"Thank you for sticking up for me, Ciaran," said Bethan, patting his arm. "But there's no point starting a fight with him. I'd prefer to just ignore him next time, especially with his threat about reporting us."

"But safety's the first thing we think about on every activity," said Bez. "He hasn't got a leg to stand on."

"We have had a couple of funny things happen recently."

"I bet that was Rhys," exclaimed Bez. "The kayaks on the trailer the other day – he could have done something with the ties overnight. And the slashed tyres this morning. Somebody obviously cut them. I wouldn't put it past him."

"I can't believe Rhys would do anything like that," said Bethan, shaking her head. "He may be a bit over-bearing sometimes but he's not malicious."

"He certainly seems malicious enough to me," Bez replied.

"Let's not talk about Rhys all night," Bethan said, shaking her head. "What were we talking before?"

They forced themselves to talk about more palatable topics, but Rhys Jones still cast his shadow across the evening. As a newcomer, Dan hadn't felt it was his place to say anything, but he was of the same mind as Ciaran. He felt that Jones could easily be responsible for the incidents that had occurred. Dan wondered why the man was so interested in buying Bethan's house. He resolved to find out.

17. Incident At Porthclais. St Davids. Friday Morning.

When Dan got out of bed the next morning and opened the curtains, there were streaks of ochre and vermillion across the sky – striking, ominous portents of the day's weather.

An hour later their party was aboard the minibus and Dan and Bez were driving towards Porthclais, a few miles south-west of St Davids. The sky above them was getting darker by the minute. Dan was sure it would rain soon.

Looking out at the countryside they were driving through, Dan was once again reminded of Cornwall. Two lands separated by a wide expanse of water, but formed in the same manner by geology and weather conditions. The occasional buildings they passed were built from slate in a similar style and sporadically a small stunted tree would struggle to grow up out of a hedgerow like an inverted L pointing inland away from the hard Atlantic winds.

They arrived at the tiny settlement of Porthclais and pulled into a small car park beside a stream that flowed down to the sea a couple of hundred yards away. The land rose up either side of them covered with a patchwork blanket of gorse and bracken.

As they got out of the minibus, Dan felt a few spots of rain start to fall. The red sky was being proved correct.

"Great," muttered Bez, looking up at the darkening sky "It always rains when I come out here. It's ridiculous."

However he put on a brave face as he turned to the customers who were climbing out of the vehicle.

"The forecast is for a few showers today guys," Bez announced, "but it won't bother us. It's just another part of nature's rich tapestry. Okay, has anyone climbed before?"

Dan glanced around. There were six customers in the group, three men, two women and a teenage boy. The teenager put his hand up shyly and announced that he had been to a party once at an indoor climbing warehouse.

Bez set everybody's mind at ease, assuring them that they were in safe hands and explained what was ahead of them.

Bez and Dan then started allocating helmets and harnesses to the group.

"Okay," Bez said loudly to attract everyone's attention again as they finished sorting out the equipment. "We're going to head up the track over there and climb up the hill on the left side of the inlet. It's only a few hundred yards to the spot where we'll be climbing. Can each of you carry your helmets and harnesses - and can a couple of you grab a rope as well please."

He asked Dan to bring up the rear and Bez led the group up the pathway.

The footpath meandered along the edge of the gorse bushes overlooking the stream as it widened out to form a small inlet on its way to the sea. Most of the party didn't seem too perturbed by the poor weather, but the young woman just in front of him was hunched inside her coat with her hood pulled tight around her head.

The path started to rise up the hill and became slightly wider so Dan took the opportunity to walk alongside her.

"It should be good fun today, despite the weather," he said breezily.

She glanced up at him quickly before lowering her head to face the ground again. "I don't know why I agreed to do it," she moaned quietly. "I might just watch actually. Or I could just go and sit in the minibus."

"You might as well give it a go now," Dan said. "Bez will look after you."

"I'm only here because my boyfriend made me come," she admitted as they continued trudging up the hill.

Dan was surprised. "Where's your boyfriend then?" he asked.

"He's up there at the front, chatting to the other instructor. What did he say he was called? Bez?"

"Yes, that's right. I'm Dan, by the way," he said, as they negotiated a stile and set off up the hill again.

"I'm Trisha. We're from Bristol. I saw this climbing thing advertised and I got it for Paul – that's my husband – for his birthday. But he said I should come too. I don't know why, if he's not even going to talk to me."

The path was nearing the top of the hill now and Dan could see the turquoise of the ocean ahead of them.

"Well you don't have to do it if you don't want to," said Dan, "but Bez knows what he's doing. He's taken loads of parties up here before. And you never know, you might enjoy it."

"I don't think so," she replied morosely. "I can't stand heights."

They arrived at the top of the hill and walked over to the rest of the party who were gathered in a jumble of boulders and stones that obviously marked the top of the cliff. The sea seemed to be a long way below them.

The group set their equipment on the ground and one of the men edged towards the cliff and looked over.

"Bloody hell," he said as he turned back with a grin.

Dan and Trisha put their kit down too and joined the others looking over the edge. Trisha sidled very slowly and cautiously towards it and Dan kept a hand free in case he needed to grab her quickly. They both looked over together just as a wave crashed against the foot of the cliff sending white foam spiralling into the air.

"Oh my God," said Trisha weakly and stepped back. Dan kept watching as another wave smashed against the rocks below. It definitely looked a long way down. At the base of the cliff about two metres above the level of the sea was a ledge and he estimated it was four or five feet wide. The waves weren't reaching the ledge, but the spray certainly was.

"Okay, everybody," shouted Bez. "Gather round please."

The group filtered over to stand around the instructor.

"As I said at the minibus, we're all going to abseil down to the ledge one at a time and then we'll climb back up. This cliff is good for beginners as it's a few degrees off the vertical, but the drizzle will make it a little more challenging. You'll be okay though. There are two main climbing routes for beginners so we'll have two groups of three coming back up. Obviously just one person climbing at a time, with Dan and I holding the safety rope."

Bez then explained the process for abseiling and gave a quick demonstration from the top of a boulder.

"Now," he continued, "your rope will be attached to this spike here, which has been driven about a metre into the rock so you're quite safe. However a second rope will also be attached to you for the abseiling which I will be managing just in case you're going a little too fast. And as you can see, I'm attached to this second spike over here." Bez's harness was clipped to a shorter rope that he now attached to another iron spike that had been driven into the rock.

"I normally run a group of six by myself," Bez continued, "but I thought it would be nice to bring Dan along today, partly to help carry the kit but primarily to be my guinea pig." He smiled at Dan.

Oh yes, thought Dan. What's going to happen now?

"Dan will go first and show us how it's done," said Bez. "Come on, let's get you roped up."

Bez lead Dan to the cliff and made him stand a few feet from the edge, facing back towards the group. Bez set up the rope and showed Dan how to control it.

"Okay, Danny boy," he said, "walk backwards and put your feet on the edge." Dan did as he was told and tried to look confident, but when he was standing with his toes on the brink of the cliff he realised his heart was racing. He tried not to look down.

"As you can see, Dan is quite relaxed," said Bez, smiling at him. "Now, I want you to lean back to about forty-five degrees. This is the tricky part if you haven't done it before."

Dan leaned back a little and glanced at the rope to make sure it looked strong enough to hold him. It seemed complete madness to be leaning back over a huge drop with the ocean thundering below him.

"A little further," coaxed Bez. Dan leaned a little more.

"Further …"

"Further … okay hold it there." Bez continued his instruction while Dan tried to look relaxed, suspended over a sixty foot drop by a rope that he now decided looked quite thin. "So, he's at about forty-five degrees. If you were more upright than this then your feet would slip down the rock as you set off and your face would bang into the cliff. You don't want that. You also don't want to lean so far back that you're horizontal. Now, the next step is to move one of your feet down the rock face slightly. Please demonstrate, Dan."

Dan looked at Bez as though he was mad, but the other man was simply smiling back at him, obviously amused. Dan didn't know what was louder: the waves crashing into the rocks sixty feet below him or his heart pounding the blood through his ears.

He lifted his foot and moved it twelve inches down the rock face.

"Now move the other foot down," said Bez. Dan did as he was told.

"Now another step," said Bez. Dan did it again, feeling ever so slightly more comfortable about what he was doing.

"Okay, keep walking down like that," Bez told him. "And if you fancy it then try a few jumps." He turned back to the group. "As you can see, the worst part is leaning out over the edge and the very first step. After that you can relax and start to have fun."

The group were all peering over watching Dan as he walked half a dozen more steps down the rock face and then paused. He tried a small jump back from the cliff and allowed the rope to slide through his hand. He dropped slowly and swung back towards the rock, cushioning himself with his legs. He jumped again, dropping a little further this time.

The third time he pushed back off the stone as hard as he could and let the rope run quickly. He felt like he was soaring like one of the seagulls that were swooping around him. He performed a couple more exhilarating leaps and then all too soon he was at the base of the cliff.

Bez shouted down instructions for Dan to detach himself from his own rope and the safety rope. The ropes were then pulled back up for the next person.

Dan looked around at the ledge, which was wider and more accommodating that it had looked from above. It ran twenty or thirty yards in each direction and was about the width of a pavement running alongside a road. He hadn't ever fallen off a pavement so why should he fall off this shelf of rock? The only problem was that every few seconds a wave hurled itself onto the rocks a few feet below and showered him with spray.

He looked up to see if the next person was starting their descent, but nobody was in sight yet. In the lull between the crashing waves he heard some voices but couldn't make out what they were saying.

The stone face of the cliff towered above him and he noticed that it leaned away from him as it ascended. Dan judged that it was about ten degrees off vertical and he realised that should make the climb slightly easier.

He heard voices above him again and a figure backed out until their heels were protruding out into the air. For a long time, the person didn't move and occasionally he caught a few snatches of Bez's soothing tones. The instructor finally persuaded the person to lean backwards a little and, after a further exchange, the lean became more pronounced.

Dan saw that it was a woman and then, with surprise, realised that it was Trisha, the girl who had professed a fear of heights as they had walked up the footpath. Bez had obviously noticed her anxiety and had elected to send her first – before she decided she wasn't going.

With further coaxing Trisha finally achieved an angle of lean that was acceptable to Bez and she slowly slid her left foot a few inches down the rock. She then slid her right foot down so that it was level with the other foot. She repeated the process slowly, but he faintly heard Bez's voice again saying "lean out more" and realised that whilst she was moving her feet, Trisha had been holding tightly onto the rope and was in danger of becoming almost vertical again.

Infinitesimally she increased her angle of lean again and then repeated the process of edging her feet down the rock. This time however she managed to allow the rope to run through slightly as well. Trisha continued walking down the cliff face, slowly but surely increasing her speed.

When she was about halfway down, she paused for a short rest and Bez shouted down to her: "Try a little jump, but don't forget to let the rope run a little too."

There's no way she's going to do a jump, thought Dan. Then to his surprise, Trisha did indeed jump gently backwards from the cliff wall and, with a huge shriek, she dropped a few feet and crashed back into the rock, more on the side of her body than on her feet.

Over a few painful seconds, Bez encouraged her to get her feet back in front of her in the right position. Then once again, she leaped backwards with a piercing scream and dropped half a dozen feet before bumping back against the stone. This time she more or less landed on her feet.

For a third time, she positioned herself carefully and launched backwards into the air with a screech, which this time sounded more like a squeal of delight to Dan's ear.

In this ungainly staccato fashion Trisha travelled down the cliff until she landed next to Dan in a crumpled heap, breathing hard. She looked up at him, her face flushed and breathed: "That was amazing." She took another couple of deep breaths. "It was like flying. I've never been more scared in my life, but I want to do it again."

Dan laughed and heard Bez whooping from high above him.

"Awesome, Trisha," he shouted from the clifftop. "Are you okay?"

"She wants to do it again," Dan shouted back and started to help her up. There was another whoop from Bez followed by cheering and applause from the others who were still poking their heads over the lip of the cliff.

Dan helped Trisha disentangle herself from the ropes and they were hauled back up. Over the next twenty minutes the remainder of the party abseiled down with varying degrees of proficiency.

The last to make the descent was Trisha's husband Paul who started well but then seemed to lose his nerve and for about five minutes remained motionless a couple of yards from the top. Eventually Bez persuaded him to continue but he walked – or rather edged – very slowly the whole way to the bottom. Bez suggested jumping a couple of times, but Paul ignored him and just continued walking down carefully.

Finally he reached the ledge where the rest of the party was gathered and they all congratulated him despite his unhurried descent. Everyone knew how hard it was to come down the cliff at whatever speed.

After he had detached himself from the ropes, Paul turned to Trisha and said: "That was terrible, wasn't it?"

"I loved it," she replied with a huge grin and her husband gave her a cross look, but Dan wondered if perhaps he was just annoyed with himself.

Bez had now pulled the ropes up and they all raised their heads to watch him come down. In three gigantic bounces and almost the same number of seconds, the instructor landed lightly on his toes beside the group.

After a few minutes for people to rest, Bez explained to the party the best approach for climbing, how to keep three points on the rock at all times and only move one hand or one foot at a time. He indicated the best routes for beginners and split people into two groups.

Bez set up the rope for the first climber in Dan's group and showed Dan how to keep the rope tight. One person from each group then began climbing with Bez and Dan belaying. The rain was still falling steadily, but nobody seemed to notice it any more.

As each person in Dan's group reached the top, Bez helped set up the rope for the next person. However the climbers in Bez's group seemed slightly more confident and soon his three climbers were all safely at the top.

Dan's group had Trisha as the second climber and she made good, but steady, progress and reached the top a few seconds after Bez's final climber had got there. That left Paul as the final person in Dan's group.

"I'll set you up Paul," said Bez, starting to loop the rope through the carabiner that was clipped to his harness. "And I'll climb up at the same time as you. That way, we can give each other a hand if we need it."

Dan smiled at the tactful way that his colleague had put it. Bez was obviously expecting Paul to need some assistance and Dan wondered if he had set up the groups like this deliberately.

"Don't worry, Bez, I'll be fine," Paul replied, not wanting to lose face any more.

With Dan holding his belay rope, Paul tentatively set off with Bez suggesting good handholds and footholds for him from below. When Paul was a dozen feet up from the ledge and starting to get a little more nervous, Bez almost ran up the rock to a point where he was a couple of metres to Paul's left.

Bez was climbing with a safety rope but he managed it himself using an ascender device which he ratcheted up each time he moved up the cliff.

Paul continued up the cliff face methodically with the instructor continuing to indicate good handholds. Dan made sure that he pulled the rope tight whenever Paul made a move.

Bez kept encouraging Paul and assuring him that he was doing well, but when he was about halfway up the cliff, Paul reached for a handhold that made him stretch a long way to his right. Just as his fingers were closing around the protruding rock, he lost his balance and fell off the cliff with a huge shout.

Dan took the strain as the rope caught the man's fall, but Paul swung from side to side like a pendulum, his knees and elbows banging against the stone as he scrabbled to get a hold again.

"You don't have to grab at the rock if you don't want to," shouted Bez. "Just protect yourself and let yourself come to a stop naturally."

Paul followed his advice, grabbed hold of the rope with both hands and soon he had stopped swinging.

"Well done," said Bez. "Now see if you can put your right hand in that small fissure just above your head. That should be a good one."

"I'm not sure if I can reach it," said Paul without even looking, obviously not wanting to take his hands off the rope.

"Come on Paul, you can do it mate. Just above your head and slightly to the right."

Paul looked up to see where the hold was and gingerly took his right hand off the rope. He reached up and curled his fingers into the gap.

"Well done, mate," came Bez's soothing voice. He then indicated another handhold and two decent footholds and Paul was back in control of his climb. Just about.

"Awesome Paul," Bez said encouragingly. "Don't worry, we all come off sometimes. That's what the safety rope is there for." He looked down and shouted: "Keep it tight, Dan."

Dan levered the rope up again and pulled it as tight as he could. He felt as though the rope caught on something and he pulled it again, even harder.

And then suddenly he felt the tightness disappear and he saw the rope go slack in front of his eyes. The line fell from the top of the cliff, as though in slow motion, and poured down into a coil at his feet. It had obviously come apart at the clifftop and the other half of rope fell down onto Paul looping itself around his shoulders.

Paul was confused for a couple of seconds and then it dawned on him that he was thirty feet up a cliff with no safety rope, just holding on with his fingers and toes.

However Bez had grasped what was happening before him and was already traversing towards Paul, once again moving with spider-like swiftness.

"Oh my God," shouted Paul, just as Bez was reaching him. He was clinging on to the rock and trying to hug it towards him. "The rope's snapped. The rope's snapped."

"It's okay, Paul," said Bez calmly. "Just relax, mate. I'm going to clip your rope onto me."

The other end of Paul's rope was of course still attached to his harness. Bez unlooped the rope from round Paul's shoulders and started attaching it to his own harness.

All the time he was talking calmly and confidently to Paul: "You just relax and concentrate on holding onto those handholds. They're good ones – nice and deep. I'm tying you onto the carabiner on my harness now." He was working with the rope as he talked. "This is a standard daisy chain system that climbers use to tie themselves to each other. I'm going to leave about three metres between us so that you've got room to climb."

"I'm not climbing any more," insisted Paul.

"Well we're not going to stay here, mate," smiled Bez. "Don't worry, I'll look after you."

"I want to go down," said Paul.

"Unfortunately that's not an option, Paul. There's just the sea down there. We'll start heading up in a minute and I'll help you every step of the way." He finished tying off the rope and put his hand back on the rock. "Okay, Paul, we've got you tied on now, you're safe. Just relax for a moment and get your breath back and in a minute we'll start climbing up."

"But the rope can't hold us both," Paul whimpered.

"These ropes can hold far more than our weight. I've seen some of them tested holding a car."

"Why did my rope snap then?"

"We'll take a look at it when we're at the top," Bez replied, not wanting to start a debate at that point. "Okay let's get moving. There's a good foothold by your right knee. Lift your foot up to that. You can do it."

It took Paul a little while to be persuaded to start moving again, but eventually he lifted his foot up. With Bez indicating the best holds, he inched his way up the face of the cliff.

Meanwhile Dan picked up the rope that had landed at his feet and examined the end. There was a smooth cut through three quarters of the diameter and the last few strands looked like they had been stretched until they had snapped. To his un-expert eye it seemed as though someone had sliced partway through, leaving enough to give the impression that the rope was sound.

Bez continued encouraging, persuading and nudging Paul up the climb until finally they reached the top. Paul got his arms over the edge and then, with help from the rest of the group, levered his body over as well. He lay there on his front, breathing hard and Trisha knelt down next to him and hugged him.

Bez detached Paul's rope from his carabiner and made sure the group were well away from the edge. He abseiled back down to where Dan was waiting at the foot of the cliff so he could belay him up.

On reaching the ledge, Bez picked up the fallen rope and examined the end like Dan had. "It looks like it's been cut to me," Bez said. "What do you think?"

"That's what it looked like to me as well. Could it have been cut on a rock up there or on the spike?"

"No way. If it was on a rock there would be fraying around the area where the cut was. And it wasn't attached directly to the spike it was on a carabiner. It looks like a knife to me."

"Just before it went, I felt like it had caught on something and I pulled on it hard. Do you think I might have snapped it by doing that?"

"Maybe," said Bez thoughtfully. "Paul coming off a few seconds before probably weakened it and maybe your pull was the final straw." He glanced up at the top of the cliff. "Anyway let's get out of here and get these people back to base."

-o-o-o-

Bez belayed Dan up the climb and then followed him up. The group quietly carried the equipment back down to the minibus and drove back to Alun House.

By the time they got there and finished explaining everything to Bethan, Paul had completely recovered and had become extremely angry. While the rest of the customers headed off and Trisha stood by silently, he threatened to refer the matter to the police and then promised to sue Bez, Bethan and even Dan.

When Bez told him it looked like the rope had been deliberately cut, Paul shouted at him that he should have checked the equipment before letting unsuspecting members of the public use it. Bez insisted that he had inspected the ropes that morning, but couldn't avoid admitting that he must have missed the cut somehow.

Eventually Paul left, promising that his solicitors would be in touch.

"Ungrateful bloke," said Bez indignantly as Paul and Trisha's car sped away. "I practically saved his life and then spent ages coaxing him up the rest of the climb when he was too scared to move."

"Well we did endanger his life in the first place," said Bethan.

"It wasn't my fault," replied Bez heatedly. "Somebody had deliberately cut that rope but only partly so that it would give way on a climb."

"It does look like it's been cut," agreed Bethan.

"I bet it was Rhys." Bez was getting worked up now. "He probably sneaked in during the night."

"It might not have been cut deliberately. It might have got snagged on something in the van."

"Come off it, Bethan. It's a perfect cut."

"Well what can we do about it? We don't have any proof it was Rhys. We can't even prove that it was done deliberately."

Bez shrugged. "I don't know what we can do about it, Bethan, but I'm sure it was him though."

"All we can do is check things even more thoroughly from now on," she replied. "Anyway we've got other things to worry about now. The weather's getting worse and we've got other activities to sort out this afternoon."

Bethan and Bez started sorting out the paperwork and inspecting the equipment for the next group, but Dan took the opportunity to slip upstairs to his room. He wanted to get on his laptop and find out a little more about Rhys Jones.

18. All Roads Lead To Haverfordwest. Angle to St Davids. Friday Morning.

That same morning Andrew and Jess drove out of Angle, backtracking a few miles up the peninsula below Milford Haven to the small town of Pembroke.

This ancient county town had grown up around the magnificent medieval castle which was constructed on a rocky promontory protruding into a lake fed by the Pembroke river. Pembroke was a nicer place than Andrew had expected – not the industrial settlement he had anticipated on the shores of Milford Haven, but the historic main street of the town hosted dozens of shops, pubs and cafes and Andrew decided to stop and ask around.

He gave Jess one of the large photos of Cullen and asked her to work along one side of the street. He took the other side.

-o-o-o-

The first place on Jess' side of the street was The Rising Sun Café. More of a *caff* she thought to herself as she went in and caught the tempting aroma of bacon and eggs. There were half a dozen people in the café eating breakfast or having a cup of tea.

"I'm looking for a man," she said to the burly owner who was squirting ketchup onto some white sliced bread. She put the photograph on the counter.

"Well you've found one, darlin'," the man replied, puffing his chest out. His accent was more East End of London than Pembroke.

"No, I'm looking for this man." Jess pointed to the photograph.

The man glanced at the picture and looked up again. "What do you want him for? He looks a bit of a tiddler. How about a real man?" He puffed his chest out again.

"His hair might be a bit darker now and slightly shorter," Jess continued, ignoring the man's responses. He was friendly enough and she was used to comments like these. "He normally calls himself Dan something. He's about six foot and thirteen stone or so. Have you seen him?"

"Nope." The man shook his head, glancing at the photograph again. "Never seen him, luv."

"Okay thanks for your help," Jess said.

"No problem," he replied, turning to the griddle and scooping up the bacon and eggs on a spatula.

Jess walked to the door.

"Hey, darlin'," the man shouted just as she was about to leave.

"Yes?" she said hopefully, thinking he might have remembered something.

"If you don't find him then come on back here. I finish at five tonight."

-o-o-o-

A couple of hours later Jess and Andrew re-convened at the car.

"Any joy?" asked Andrew.

"No," Jess replied, shaking her head. "And I'm exhausted now."

"Let's go." Andrew got into the car.

Jess jumped in and Andrew drove out of Pembroke heading north to the long toll bridge which would take them across to the other side of the estuary.

"Did you look at their eyes like I told you?" Andrew asked as he negotiated his way around a roundabout.

"Of course I did," Jess replied testily.

"Let me explain again, just in case. There's no harm in a quick recap now that you've asked a few people. Eyes going up and to the left indicates visually constructed images, meaning they are lying, whereas up and right indicates visually remembered images. The trouble is, if they're left-handed then it's the other way round. And of course it's only a guide."

"Don't worry, I've got it," sighed Jess. "Up and to the left means they're lying. Unless they're left-handed."

"Also looking left or eyes de-focussing or avoiding eye contact, but also touching or scratching their face, timing of gestures could seem slightly off or the whole combination of things. Anyway I don't expect you to be a lie detection expert. Ask them the question, look at their reactions and just give me a shout if something seems a bit funny. Most of these people have come to like Stephen Cullen and their natural reaction might be protective."

"The biggest problem," said Jess pensively, "is that they want to know why we're looking for this man. And then you spend five minutes trying to get away."

"Just tell them that it's confidential and move on. There's no time to have a long discussion with everybody."

Jess nodded, looking out of the window as they crossed the estuary over a long bridge.

"Can I ask you a question?" said Jess.

"You just have," said Andrew.

"What would you do with a million pounds?" she asked.

"I'd give it away."

She turned to look at him. "You're serious?"

"Aye, it would only cause trouble. And I have enough money."

"Have you paid off your mortgage?"

"No."

"Well, would you want to?"

"I'll pay it off over the next fifteen years. My salary is enough to cover that and whatever else I need."

"You must be quite parsimonious."

"I'm not sure if that is a compliment these days, but I would say that I am."

At the far side of the estuary they followed the road to Haverfordwest.

"Do you want to know what I would do with a million pounds?" Jess asked.

"Buy lots of shoes?"

Jess laughed. "Do you think that all women like shoes?" she said.

Andrew glanced over at her and raised an eyebrow.

"Okay," she smiled. "I'd buy a few pairs of shoes. And I'd pay off my parents' mortgage and maybe buy myself a place round here. But most of all I'd want a TVR Tuscan convertible."

"I presume that's a car?"

"Yes a British-made sports car," Jess said. "Hey, you know you said you'd give the million pounds away?"

"Yes," said Andrew.

"That's what Cullen did."

Andrew ignored the point and concentrated on his driving. He saw a sign to Little Haven and turned off the main road. They travelled a few miles along winding country roads without speaking for a while.

Presently Jess turned to look at him. "Andrew?" she said.

"Yes ...?" replied Andrew warily, expecting another silly question.

"I know you want to be methodical, but it's going to take ages to go round all of the places in Pembrokeshire."

"We're not covering all of Pembrokeshire. We're initially going to places that support casual labour, primarily tourist locations along the coast."

"But the coast is pretty long," Jess argued. "Why don't we go up to St Davids? I had a look on the internet last night and I found three or four outdoor sports businesses there."

"It's forty-five minutes drive up to St Davids. And if he's not there, then what? Drive all the way back down here again? We can't zigzag haphazardly all over south Wales – it will take twice as long."

"But I feel like he's there. In St Davids I mean."

Andrew snorted. "Only because I told you that yesterday," Andrew said. "St Davids is perhaps the prime spot, but all of these other seaside places along the way are good candidates as well and he could easily be in any one of them. We need to cover them all in the most efficient manner."

Jess conceded with a shrug of her shoulders, "Okay, you're the boss."

"If it's any consolation I'm hoping that we'll be up at St Davids by the end of the day. We're heading north up St Brides Bay and there are half a dozen places for us to check out along the way – but St Davids is at the top of the bay."

Jess nodded and settled back in her seat.

-o-o-o-

Fifteen minutes later they came down the hill into the small settlement of Little Haven. Andrew could see a small bay ahead of them through the houses. He drove slowly into the village.

"What a strange little place," he said, glancing around. "There are more pubs and cafes than houses. It must be busy in the summer."

"I remember coming here on our coastal walk," said Jess. "It was busy, but it's a lovely place."

He parked in the small car park and they set off to ask at the pubs and cafés for Cullen. Unfortunately they had a negative response in each place they tried and were soon back in the car.

Just a couple of minutes after leaving Little Haven the road swung back towards the sea and they came down into the village of Broad Haven.

"This place is aptly named," Andrew said, looking down the sea front. "It's certainly broader than Little Haven – much bigger in fact. And there are quite a few more shops and pubs."

They parked halfway along the seafront and agreed that Jess would go in one direction, whilst Andrew would go in the other. They set off just as a light rain started to fall. Andrew looked up at the sky and saw dark clouds to the north.

By early afternoon they were back at the car again, dispirited and wet. Once again, Cullen had not been seen anywhere.

As they climbed up the road on the northern side of Broad Haven, there was a sign to the right for Haverfordwest and straight ahead was Nolton Haven.

-o-o-o-

They stopped for a quick bite to eat at the solitary Mariners Inn which overlooked the shy, unobtrusive bay of Nolton Haven and then drove on to its more ebullient elder brother – the long, windswept beach of Newgale. A handful of cafes and shops had been sprinkled haphazardly along this three mile stretch of coastline and Andrew stopped obsessively at each one – he was scared to miss one out in case it was *the* one – but once again they had no success.

"This beach is different to all the others," Andrew said as they came towards the northern end of Newgale. "This is the only beach that has a bank of pebbles that runs the whole way along." The tide was out and the wide sandy beach gave way to the stones which rose to form a storm bank and then fell away to the road. On the other side of the road, grass-covered dunes rose up to the hills in the distance.

They came to a point where the road descended slightly to cover a two hundred yard dip where pebbles were on both sides of the road. The road had recently been re-surfaced here indicating that the sea had caused some damage over the winter. The newly laid tarmac looked like it had simply been unrolled across the pebbles like a black carpet.

The stones along the beach were a myriad of different colours. Many of the pebbles which had been rounded by the sea over thousands of years were fashioned from the slate that was indigenous to this whole area of Wales, but they exhibited innumerable shades of gray – and Jess noticed that they even showed hints of other colours. A deep red-grey was particularly commonplace.

"Look at the colour of the stones – some of them are a plummy sort of colour," Jess said to Andrew.

"Are they?" he replied, staring hard. "They just look like normal stone colours to me."

Jess shrugged and they drove on still looking at the scenery around them.

Jess noticed the occasional stunted tree beside the road which was hunched against the prevailing wind which came in from the Atlantic. The wind had now strengthened and the rain had returned, more heavily than before.

At the top of St Brides Bay, they came to another fork in the road where a signpost once again indicated Haverfordwest to the right. They turned left towards St Davids and after a mile found themselves in a large village called Solva.

Although the open sea was not visible due to the surrounding hills, the village was situated at the top of a meandering tidal inlet and its pleasant location meant it was able to support a modest number of pubs, shops and even an art gallery specialising in local landscapes.

They stopped to show the photograph of Cullen around the village in the pouring rain. Once again they had no success and returned like drowned rats to the car.

-o-o-o-

It was nearly six o'clock when they came into St Davids and most of the shops were now closed for the day.

"Let's check into a hotel before we ask around at the pubs," said Andrew.

"What?" said Jess in surprise. "Pubs? Don't we get the evening off?"

"You said you wanted to look for Cullen in St Davids. We're here now."

"But I've said 'have you seen this man?' a thousand times today and I need a rest. Aren't you fed up with it too?"

"No," replied Andrew as though he didn't even understand why she was asking the question.

"I don't even think that he's in Wales any more. We'll never find him – he's too clever to be caught."

"You're very negative," Andrew said indignantly. "We'll catch him. It might not be today, it might not be tomorrow, but he'll make a mistake and I'll catch him. Nobody steals that much money and is able to hide forever."

"I'm impressed by your confidence, Andrew, but I have to admit that I don't share it."

"We'll find a hotel, rest for an hour and then ask around the pubs and other hotels. It looks like there are less than a dozen. And we'll do the shops and other places in the morning. And your outdoor activities places."

They pulled into the central square of the city with a pub called The Bishops on one side and The Old Cross Hotel on another side.

Andrew pulled into the hotel car park and they went into reception. Jess breathed a sigh of relief when the receptionist said that the hotel had two rooms for them.

-o-o-o-

An hour later they met back down in reception to start the evening shift in their hunt for Cullen.

"Sorry I was so negative earlier," said Jess, as they walked out of the hotel. "I was a bit tired."

"This shouldn't take more than an hour anyway. We can finish at that pub." He indicated The Bishops on the other side of the square. "We can eat there perhaps."

They started walking down the road.

"When we did the coast walk we had a pizza in a little restaurant over that side of town I think." Jess pointed over to the left. "And stayed at a bed and breakfast round the corner from it. We had a great time on that walk," she added wistfully. "In my mind, every single day was sunshine and deep blue skies, but we must have had some bad days I suppose."

"Did you say you did the walk with your husband?" Andrew asked tentatively.

"Yes. Well he was my boyfriend at the time, but we got married a few months later." Her voice tailed away towards the end and she looked down at her feet as they continued walking down the road.

After a couple of seconds, Andrew said: "Has your husband moved down to London with you?"

"Oh no," she replied, still looking downwards. "We split up just before Christmas."

"I'm sorry to hear that," said Andrew, but then he realised he was actually quite pleased.

"These things don't work out sometimes. When you get married, you think it's going to be forever, but I suppose it wasn't meant to be."

Andrew didn't know what to say. He never knew what to say in these circumstances.

"That's part of the reason why I left the police and moved down to London," Jess continued. "I just wanted to get away from it all. Get away from him, I suppose I mean. And his friends. Newcastle can be a small place sometimes."

They continued strolling slowly down the road and without really noticing it walked through a large stone archway. As the thoroughfare opened out again they suddenly realised they were looking down on the magnificent sight of St Davids Cathedral nestling in a small, sheltered valley to the right of the road. Behind it was the equally impressive Bishops Palace.

The rain had stopped and the evening sun was glinting off the walls of the cathedral picking out the colours of the stone and highlighting the stained glass windows.

"They tucked that huge building away quite well, didn't they," said Jess as they stopped to take in the sight before them.

Andrew nodded slowly. "I suppose they didn't want to attract too much attention in those times. There were always invading armies looking to take whatever they could find, even from religious sites. You wouldn't want to put a defenceless cathedral full of rich artefacts on top of a hill where everyone could see it."

Jess nodded and pointed to the western end of the building. "The stone of the cathedral is interesting," she said. "That section looks like it was added later, the stones are larger and are the same plummy coloured slate that we saw on that beach."

Andrew stared at the cathedral. "It doesn't look plum coloured to me. Dark grey."

Jess sighed. Suddenly she turned away from him. "Okay, without looking at me, what colour are my eyes?"

"That's easy," said Andrew. "They're light brown with flecks of darker brown."

"Not bad." Jess was impressed. She turned back towards him.

"It's my job to notice things about people," Andrew shrugged.

"In that much detail?"

"Er … we should really get to work." Andrew took out two sheets of paper from his pocket. "I picked up a couple of street maps from the hotel and marked them up while I was waiting for you in reception. We'll do half of the streets each as usual and then meet back in The Bishops pub." Andrew handed a map to Jess and marched off.

-o-o-o-

Fifty minutes later Andrew entered The Bishops and glanced around. There were a good number of people in the pub but it didn't look like Jess was here.

He walked up to the bar and waited until the barmaid had finished serving a customer. When the girl came over, he showed her the photograph of Cullen. "Excuse me," he said, "could you tell me if you've seen this man?"

The barmaid glanced at the picture and then looked more closely. "He looks familiar," she said slowly. Andrew leaned forward eagerly – could this be the breakthrough they had been searching for? After a couple more seconds of staring at the photo, the barmaid turned and called to her colleague who was working behind the bar with her. The young man came over and she asked him to look at the photograph as well.

"Nope," said the barman after a moment. "I haven't seen him. Who is he?"

"I'm afraid I can't say. I work for an investigative agency and we've simply been charged with finding this man. By the way, his hair might be a different colour now. He's approximately six feet tall and thirteen and a half stone with an athletic build. He might be going by the first name Dan, but he changes his surname regularly."

The girl stared at the photo again. "I do feel like I've seen him, but I can't remember where." She looked up at Andrew again. "Why are you looking for him? Is he dangerous?"

Andrew had been asked the same question many times that day, but he replied as civilly as he could: "We have no reason to believe that he is dangerous and I'm afraid I can't divulge the reason we're looking for him. Where do you think you might have seen him? In this pub?"

"Maybe," she said, pursing her lips and looking up at the ceiling for inspiration.

Andrew turned to the barman, who was looking at the photograph again. "Are you sure you haven't seen him?"

"I don't think so." The young man shook his head.

He turned back to the barmaid. "Do you think you might have seen him recently?" Andrew asked her.

"Maybe," she replied and then shrugged her shoulders as if admitting defeat. "I don't know. I can't remember."

"Did you see him today?"

"No," she replied with a little more conviction. "I'm pretty sure it wasn't today. But not ages ago either."

"Were you working here yesterday?"

"Yes."

Andrew turned to the barman. "Were *you* working here yesterday?"

"No, I've been away for a week. Just got back today."

Andrew turned back to the barmaid. "Have you been working here all week?"

"I had the day off on Tuesday, but I've done every evening since last Sunday."

"Do you think you might have seen him in the last week? It would seem likely if you think you've seen the man, but your colleague hasn't."

"Maybe. No. Yes. Oh I don't know," she said shaking her head. "It's pretty busy in here most nights. We get a lot of customers."

"But at this time of year it's mostly locals isn't it?" Andrew asked.

"It is quieter at this time of year," the girl replied, "but there are always new faces in the pub. People do the Pembrokeshire coastal path all year round and the twitchers come here for the birds on Ramsey Island all the time."

"And there's the seals in Ramsey Sound as well," added the young barman.

Andrew decided not to push things. "Thank you for your help for now," he said and got out one of his business cards. "Here's my phone number – call me at any time day or night if you think of anything. And I was planning to have dinner here so I'll be around for the next hour or two – if you remember anything else can you let me know?"

"Sure," said the girl. "I just wish I could remember where I'd seen him."

"Don't worry about it. Sometimes reaching for memories is like chasing butterflies: they can dance out of your grasp just as you try to close your hand around them. It's better to let them come to you."

"Very poetic," said a voice next to him. It was Jess. "Has she seen him?"

"She thinks she might have done." Andrew turned back to the barmaid. "Just come and get me if you remember where you saw him."

"Okay," the girl replied. "Would you like some menus?" She fetched a pair of menus from the end of the bar. Andrew and Jess picked what they wanted, placed their order and bought some drinks.

They found a table in the corner of the pub and Andrew brought his colleague up to speed with the conversation he had just had.

"How about you? Did you get anywhere with any of the places you went to?" asked Andrew as he took a sip of his beer.

"No, nothing anywhere else," replied Jess. "But this sounds good. I hope she remembers where she saw him."

"I think she saw him recently. She couldn't articulate it herself, but I don't think a vague memory like that would have stayed with her for long. She must have seen him in the last couple of days."

"What do we do now?"

"Well, a slight change of tactics is called for now. If she has seen him recently then he's probably still in St Davids – he normally stays in one place for a week or so. And if we show the photo round all the shops in St Davids tomorrow then we might spook him into running off to another part of the country again. I think we need to try a softer approach."

"Like catching a butterfly?"

"Aye, quite so," he replied and then looked at Jess. "Are you mocking me?"

"Only a little," she smiled. "I didn't know you had it in you to be so lyrical. I do agree with your suggestion though. And your metaphor, for that matter. Or was it a simile? Anyway what do you suggest?"

"I'm not sure yet," Andrew replied pensively. "We don't want to blunder around and inadvertently show the photo to the person who is currently employing him. They'll blank us, tell Cullen and he'll disappear. It would be nice if this barmaid were able to point us in the right direction." He thought for a moment. "Cullen knows what I look like, even though it was dark when we met in Cornwall that night. Maybe I should tuck myself away in the hotel and you should be the one who looks around in the morning."

"That's fine by me," said Jess excitedly. "What do you want me to do?"

"I don't know yet. Let me think on it."

At that moment, Andrew's phone rang. He glanced down and saw that it was Vinod.

"Hello, Vinod," he said as he accepted the call. "I thought you were going to phone me in the afternoon today?"

"I tried," said Vinod in an exasperated tone. "I've been trying you every fifteen minutes since about four o'clock, but it just kept going straight to voicemail and you said I couldn't leave you a message."

"Good boy. Do you have an update for me then?"

"Yes, we've made some progress today, but we still don't know the full story. You remember I told you yesterday that we had tracked the money to these accounts for half a dozen imaginary people?"

"Aye."

"And the money had gone out of the accounts leaving just £1 in each one?"

"Aye. Come on Vinod."

"Well we've now tracked all the payments to about thirty five other accounts. There were hundreds of payments criss-crossing from the imaginary accounts to these accounts, but in total some people have received around £50,000 and others a few hundred thousand pounds."

"Are you telling me that these are real people now? Real bank accounts for real people?"

"Yes, they are. I think this is the end of the trail now. The bank accounts are normal people's bank accounts with salaries coming in once a month and the usual outgoings: gas bill, electricity, insurance, mortgage, cashpoint withdrawals, cheques. They're real people and they all live all over the UK. Scotland, Northern Ireland, Wales, London, Norfolk, Yorkshire. All over the country really."

"So why did Stephen Cullen give these people ten million pounds?"

"I'm afraid I've got no idea, Andrew."

"Are they linked to him in any way?"

"Not that I can see."

"Are they linked to each other somehow?" asked Andrew.

"We haven't found a link yet, but we spent most of the day working out the money and we only got access to their personal accounts in the last couple of hours. Well Nigel was looking at their accounts while I was starting to map out their personal details."

"Good lad. Email the records over to me when you've got all the information. I'd like to see dates of birth, address, family details, where they work, hobbies, everything. I presume you rang them and asked them about the money? What did they say?"

There was silence on the line.

"Vinod. You did ring them, didn't you?" Andrew asked again. "Even just a couple of them?"

"I didn't think of doing that."

"Why not? We are allowed to talk to people, you know. It's not all about just looking up facts and figures."

"Sorry, Andrew. Do you want me to go back to the office now and ring some of them?"

"Aye, of course I do. Hang on, why do you need to go back to the office though? You can log into the system from home."

"The details are all just on scraps of paper on my desk. I hadn't started entering them onto the system yet," Vinod said plaintively.

"Why didn't you – " he started and gave up. "How quickly can you get there?"

"Er … maybe an hour. Perhaps a little more."

"An hour?" exclaimed Andrew. "Where are you?"

"I'm at the pub with some friends. I'll need to go home and get my pass and then get the tube to the office."

"Oh, leave it until tomorrow, lad," said Andrew, exasperated. "It'll be after ten o'clock before you start ringing people." He paused. "I've got a better idea – email the names and phone numbers to me first thing in the morning and I'll ring them. I need to stay in the hotel in the morning anyway."

"Sorry, Andrew. Er, have you remembered it's Saturday tomorrow?"

"So?"

"Er, nothing. Okay. I'll get in early and send them over to you. How have you been getting on today?" asked Vinod, desperate to change the subject.

"Pretty good, I think," replied Andrew. "We're in a place called St Davids and I think he's here. This place fits the profile and we've got a barmaid who thinks she's seen him. Jess is going to look round quietly tomorrow while I stay out of the way. If he's here, Vinod, I'm going to get him."

19. Running In A Storm Of Calamity. St Davids. Saturday Morning.

Dan opened the curtains and wished he was looking at the red sky of the previous morning. Red was better than black. There were dark clouds above and rain was bouncing off the slate flagstones on the patio below his window. And it didn't look like it was going to stop soon.

He dressed and went downstairs. As he approached the kitchen he heard voices.

"So what do you think of Dan then?" he heard Bethan ask.

He paused in the corridor to hear the answer.

"He's a good lad," replied Bez's voice. "What do *you* think of him though?"

"What do you mean?" Bethan replied.

"You know what I mean. I see the way you look at him sometimes."

Dan didn't want to eavesdrop, but he wasn't sure if this was a good time to enter the kitchen either.

"That's nonsense," Bethan said and then asked. "Anyway have you made up with Kate yet?"

"You're changing the subject. But no. Anyway it's her fault."

"Whatever it is, you should apologise. You can't carry on like this."

"I'm not saying sorry first," Bez said stubbornly. "I can put up with the silent treatment for longer than she can. She'll crack soon."

Dan decided he could now enter the room safely and walked in and, pretending he hadn't heard the conversation, said briskly: "Who'll crack soon?"

"Kate," said Bez. "She's still giving me the silent treatment but I'm not giving in."

Dan poured himself some corn flakes. He sat down opposite Bethan who was drinking a cup of tea at the kitchen table.

"I found out something about Rhys yesterday," he said as he poured milk over his cereal.

Bethan and Bez looked at him. "What?" said Bez, sitting down on the other side of the table, next to Bethan. "Come on, spill the beans."

"He's short of money. He has a big overdraft, his estate agents firm has made big losses over the last couple of years and he's got some property deals with large mortgages. I couldn't look at everything he's involved in, but the stuff that I looked at was all in the red."

"How much are we talking about?" asked Bez. Bethan was staying quiet.

"His loans and mortgages total a couple of million I suppose. But of course it could be that his properties are worth a lot more than that. By the way, did you know that he owns the place next door and the plot of land the other side of that?"

"You must have got that wrong," Bethan said. "Glenys lives next door. She's lived there for fifty years."

"Well Rhys became the owner a couple of weeks ago."

"How do you know all this?" Bethan asked, still not believing him.

"I just looked up a few things up on the internet last night." Dan spooned some corn flakes into his mouth. "A lot of this information is in the public domain."

"But how can you find out stuff like that?" Bez asked.

"Well the Land Registry website will let you know who owns each property, what they paid and who their mortgage is with. And you can get annual accounts for businesses from a number of sites. His estate agency is obviously a limited company which submits accounts each year and you can see what his profit and loss was. And he's got a number of other limited companies as well."

"Hang on," said Bez. "You said a minute ago that he's overdrawn in his personal account."

"Yes, by about five thousand pounds and he's got quite a few loans as well."

"But how can you find that out?"

"Er, well I used to work at a bank." Before Bez could push him any further, Dan said: "Anyway the point is that Rhys owes a lot of money. He seems to have a lot of assets but they've all got big mortgages on them."

"So why does he want to buy Bethan's place?" said Bez.

"I've no idea," admitted Dan. "But it's interesting that he's bought the two properties next door. I was going to look into it a bit more tonight."

"I don't think it's right," said Bethan. "Looking into people's personal affairs."

"Why not?" said Bez, indignantly. "He's been sabotaging our kit – I think that gives us the right."

"I'm not so sure," said Bethan, as she stood up. "We don't really know that it was him." She put her mug in the dishwasher. "Anyway let's stop worrying about Rhys. We've got to get ready for the boat trip."

"So it's going ahead, is it?" asked Dan. "I wondered if it might be off because of the rain."

"The worst of the storm is meant to be towards the end of the day, but this morning shouldn't be too bad."

"So it's going to get worse than this?"

"Yes, there'll be strong winds tonight and a lot more rain."

"But should we be taking a boat trip out if that's the case?"

"Well people will get wet, but it's not dangerous this morning. Some of them have come a long way and we don't want to disappoint them. We give them weatherproof clothing anyway and the seals might be a bit more active in this weather. But we'll have to make sure we get them back by lunchtime."

-o-o-o-

"Look at the weather," said Jess.

It was eight thirty and Jess and Andrew had met for breakfast in the restaurant of the Old Cross Hotel. They had a table by a window and were looking out at the rain.

The waitress who had shown them to their table was now pouring Jess a cup of tea and heard her comment on the weather. "It's forecast to get worse later," she offered.

"Worse?" said Jess in surprise. "How much worse can it get?"

"This is the front of a storm that's coming in from the Atlantic and by late afternoon there should be eighty mile an hour winds and a fifteen to twenty foot swell out at sea. Maybe more." She moved round the table and poured a cup of tea for Andrew.

"You know a lot about the weather forecast," said Jess.

"My boyfriend is on the lifeboat so he looks at the forecasts every morning. He needs to be ready in case he gets a shout."

The waitress finished pouring the tea and left the pot with them.

"I'd like you to look for a job in St Davids today," said Andrew as he took a bite of his breakfast.

"Pardon?" Jess looked up at him confused.

"To look for Cullen. I'd like you to go into the shops and the adventure sports places and say that you're looking for a job. And ask if they know of anywhere that has taken people on recently."

"I see," nodded Jess. "That's a good idea."

"Of course you don't want anyone to actually offer you a job on the spot. So work out what you're going to say if that happens. Perhaps that you're not looking for work right now, but in a week's time or something like that."

"Okay. And if I hear about somewhere that took somebody on recently?"

"Call me. We might just watch them or we might go and talk to them. It depends. And keep your eyes open – it's only a small place and he might just walk past you. Look at every car that goes past as well."

Andrew's phone rang and he glanced down. It was Vinod.

"Good morning, Vinod."

"Hi Andrew. I've entered all the details of the thirty five people and I've just emailed them off to you. They're also in the case file on the system."

"Thank you," said Andrew, glancing at his watch. "You must have been up early this morning."

"I didn't want you to be cross with me again."

"You're a good lad."

"Er, Andrew?

"Aye?"

"You know how it's Saturday … is it okay if I head back home now?"

"It's okay. You can have the rest of the day off while we carry on working."

"You can call me if you need anything."

"Aye, I will Vinod. You can be sure of that."

-o-o-o-

Bethan, Bez and Dan were in the office at Alun House. Bethan was at the desk helping today's group sort out the money and paperwork for the boat trip. When each person was finished Bez and Dan were allocating them an all-in-one padded waterproof suit of the right size.

"Hi, I'm looking for Bethan Geddes," said a loud voice in the doorway, shouting across all of the people milling about.

Bethan looked up. "That's me," she said. "Would you be Radeep Addison?"

"Yes," he replied, making his way through the other customers trying on their waterproofs. A young girl of about ten years old was holding his hand. "Sorry we're late. We've driven all the way over from Reading this morning."

"Don't worry, you're the last here but you're just in time. You must have been up early though?"

"About five o'clock," Radeep nodded. "But my daughter Asha has been looking forward to this." He put his hand around her shoulders.

"Will we see seals?" Asha asked excitedly. Her father smiled.

"Yes, there's quite a few around at the moment," Bethan replied.

"Will we see dolphins?" the little girl asked.

"I'm not so sure about dolphins," Bethan told her. "We get them round here occasionally, but we haven't seen any for a while. The trip that went out yesterday saw a group of four porpoises though and they're like small dolphins." She handed some sheets of paper to the girl's father. "Could you sign these please Mr Addison. You've already paid in full but these are just our standard disclaimer. Once you've done that, please see Dan or Bez about some waterproof clothing. You're going to need it today."

Bethan turned back to her desk.

The phone rang and she picked it up. "Geddes Outdoor Sports," she said.

It was Ciaran. "Hi, Bethan," he said. "You're not going to be happy but I can't come in today. I've been ill all night."

"Hangover?" Bethan asked sarcastically. On hearing this, Bez and Dan glanced over at her.

"No, honestly, I went to bed at about eight o'clock because I was feeling so bad," said Ciaran. "I'll try to come in this afternoon if I can make it."

"Don't worry," Bethan replied. "We did have a group for climbing this afternoon but I've just cancelled them because of the weather."

"Okay. Sorry Bethan."

"Don't worry – I'll sort it out. I'll see you tomorrow though?"

"Yes, hopefully I should be okay tomorrow."

After saying goodbye, Bethan looked out of the window for a moment to think.

"Right," she said after a couple of seconds. "I'll come and do the boat with you, Bez." She turned to Dan. "Can you look after the office here, Dan?"

"Sure, what do you want me to do?"

"Just be here really. You might get people coming in off the street wanting to book something or you might get a phone call. Don't worry about emails – I'll go through them later."

She quickly showed Dan the booking management system on the computer and said: "Don't worry too much about booking them in though. The important thing is to get their name and contact details and I can give them a call back this afternoon."

"No problem."

Bethan and Bez finished sorting out the party for the boat trip and set off in the minibus.

Dan sat down at the desk and waited. He wondered if he'd landed the best job in this weather.

-o-o-o-

By mid-morning, Jess had been into nearly all the shops in the centre of St Davids, but had yet to find any clue as to Cullen's whereabouts. There were still a few places she needed to visit on the outskirts of the small city, but her last call in the centre itself was the bakery at the end of the High Street.

"Good morning," said a large lady behind the counter, with a welcoming smile.

"I wonder if you can help me?" said Jess. "I'm looking for work in St Davids. Just something part-time for a week or two."

"We're not looking for anyone I'm afraid, dear."

"Do you happen to know of anywhere that's been taking people on recently?"

"Well I suppose you could try Bethan Geddes at Geddes Outdoor Sports. They're just up the road. You might be out of luck though. She took on a young man just a couple of days ago. In here it was."

"Really?"

"I remember he came in here asking for a croissant. And then he asked for a job, but the funny thing was, he didn't want paying. Just somewhere to pitch his tent, he said. And Bethan was right behind him in the queue so she snapped him up, she did."

Jess was pleased that the woman was so talkative. "I might give her a try then," she said. "Did you say they were called Geddes Outdoor Sports?"

"Turn left out of the shop. A few hundred yards up the road on the right it is." The lady indicated the direction. "And tell her Zena sent you."

"Thanks for your help," said Jess and left the shop. She turned up the road and stopped in an office doorway to shelter from the rain while she called Andrew.

"How are you getting on?" said Andrew when he answered.

"I think I've found where he is," Jess replied enthusiastically. "I've just been into a bakery and they said that a man got a job at Geddes Outdoor Sports a couple of days ago. And listen to this: he didn't want any money, he just wanted somewhere to pitch his tent."

"That sounds like our man."

"What shall we do now?" asked Jess excitedly. "Their office is just a few hundred yards up the road. Shall I go up there?"

Andrew thought for a moment.

"Aye," he said slowly. "I think that would be a good idea. He doesn't know your face. Why don't you tell them you're looking to book an activity or find out about costs. Don't ask any questions about Cullen, just use your eyes while you're there."

"What should I do if I see him?" Jess asked.

"Don't do anything. Just finish your conversation normally and come out and call me. Once we've confirmed it's him, we call in the local police to make the arrest."

"Okay," Jess replied. She was about to hang up and then remembered that Andrew had been working on the case too. "Have you been phoning those people that Cullen gave the money to?"

"Aye, I've spoken to about half of them. Very interesting. I'll tell you all about it when you get back but I'd prefer you to get up to the Geddes office straight away."

"Okay, I'm on my way," Jess said and hung up.

-o-o-o-

Dan looked out of the office window. It was still raining heavily. In fact, it was raining *more* heavily if anything and the wind was picking up.

He looked at his watch. Nearly twelve o'clock. He hoped Bethan and Bez were okay out on the boat. He didn't think the group would be having much fun in this weather even if the seals were a bit more active.

Dan had only taken one phone call in the two hours he'd been in charge and he didn't think he'd get many people wandering in from the street with the rain pouring down.

He glanced out of the window again and was surprised to see a woman walking briskly up the drive, her hood up, her shoulders hunched against the elements.

He stood up from the desk and went to meet her at the front door.

"You'd better come in out of the rain," Dan said as she hurried into the open porch. "You can take your coat off and hang it here if you like."

Jess stepped in through the doorway before pulling her hood back and looking up at the man who was welcoming her.

"You're – " Jess almost said his name in surprise at seeing him right in front of her. She stopped herself just in time. "Er, you're … er … very kind."

Dan helped her out of her coat and hung it on the hooks in the porch. A puddle quickly formed below the coat and started running across the slate floor towards the driveway.

"Come into the office," Dan said. "I presume you're here for Geddes Outdoor Sports?"

"Yes," she said, following him through.

"Please take a seat." He indicated the chair in front of the desk. "How can I help you?"

"Er … I … we were looking to do some canoeing. I just wanted to find out the prices."

Dan handed her the price list. "This leaflet explains all the costs," he said. "Would it just be you?"

"Yes," Jess replied. "No. My partner might come along as well so it might be two of us."

"Well, the second column shows the prices if there is a party of two. Would it be this weekend?"

"Yes, tomorrow perhaps. If the rain stops." Jess stood up. She hoped the conversation had been long enough to avoid suspicion. "Anyway thank you for your help."

"Can I take a name and contact number for you?"

"Er, no, that's okay. I'll just give you a ring in the morning if we want to book something." Jess stood up.

Dan was surprised that she was leaving already, but he hardly expected to take a booking with the weather as it was. He escorted her back to the door.

Jess prepared once more to face the elements. She put her coat back on, zipped it up, popped the poppers, pulled up her hood and drew its drawstring tight around her face. She wished she hadn't taken it off in the first place.

"Thanks for your help," she said briskly and set off.

"No problem," replied Dan, but she had already gone.

He stood at the door watching her walk away and wondered if all conversations with potential customers were that brief. When the woman was halfway up the drive, she glanced back at him quickly. He held up a hand but she ignored him and turned back to continue up the driveway.

-o-o-o-

Jess decided it was too wet to stop and talk on the phone. The hotel was only a few hundred yards away so she hurried back.

At the hotel, she went straight to Andrew's room.

He opened the door, wrinkled his nose and said: "You're wet."

"Very perceptive," she said curtly as she pushed past him into the room. "I've been walking all over St Davids in the rain while you've been snuggled up in the warmth you know."

"Well take your coat off and hang it in the shower or something," said Andrew without any sympathy. "And tell me what happened."

"I saw him," she said over her shoulder as she went into the shower room and took off her coat.

"What?" said Andrew. "You saw Cullen?"

"Yes," she shouted back through to the bedroom. She looked around for somewhere to hang her coat in the bathroom and then decided to throw it on the floor of the shower. She came back into the bedroom. "He was the only one there."

"Really?" said Andrew sitting on the edge of the bed.

"It must be a small business."

"And?"

"He seemed nice," Jess said.

"Nice?" Andrew said in an exasperated voice. "He's a criminal."

"Yes, but he was nice. He welcomed me at the door and helped me take off my coat. And then he was very helpful as he talked me through the costs of kayaking."

"So if somebody's nice that's okay, is it? We can let him get away with it?"

"All I'm saying is that he didn't seem like a hard-nosed criminal to me."

"What else did you talk about?"

"Nothing. I asked about prices and then I thought I should leave before I blurted anything out. I nearly put my foot in it as it was."

"Did you?" Andrew looked at her sharply. "How?"

"Don't worry, I said 'nearly'. I had my head down when he met me at the door. I looked up and there he was. It was a bit of a shock that's all, seeing him right there in front of me. I think I covered up my surprise quite quickly though."

"Right," said Andrew standing up. "We'd better move fast in case you've spooked him. Let's get down the road to the police station."

"I didn't spook him," Jess said plaintively, not moving.

"Either way, we've found him and we need to arrest him. Now." He looked at her and moved his hand in a *hurry up* motion. "Get your coat then," he said impatiently.

Jess sighed and went to put on her wet coat yet again.

-o-o-o-

Andrew and Jess entered the small police station in St Davids.

A young police officer was just coming around the desk pulling on his coat. There was nobody else in the building.

"Can I help you?" he said as he zipped up his coat.

Andrew showed his identification card. "My name is Andrew Muir," he said. "I work for an investigative agency called DHC on behalf of the ZBS Banking Group who have engaged us to trace Stephen Cullen, a former employee who has stolen a large sum of money from the bank."

"Okay," said the policeman, with obvious impatience.

"I've located this man in St Davids and need you to arrest him. I have details about the case here from the Metropolitan Police with a copy of the warrant for his arrest. I can take you along to where the man is now."

"Is this man a threat to the public?" asked the police officer.

"No," admitted Andrew, "But why are you asking that? He's been on the run for two years and we've finally tracked him down."

"If he's not dangerous then I'm going to have to leave him for a couple of hours I'm afraid. I've got a tree down across the main road into St Davids. I was just heading there as you came in. Can you give me your phone number and I'll call you as soon as I get back?"

"No," said Andrew. "You can't put me on hold. This man has stolen ten million pounds and I need him arrested. Can I speak to your superior please? What's your name?"

"I'm PC Evans," replied the young policeman. "And I'm afraid you can't speak to my sergeant – he works on the lifeboat and he's just had a call. Apparently there's a fishing vessel in trouble about five miles offshore. They couldn't get hold of enough of the lifeboat crew so Terry had to go even though he was meant to be on duty with me."

"Is there nobody else here?"

"There's my colleague PC Morgan, but he's out at another incident and, in any case, I'm the senior officer in the absence of my sergeant. Now I'm afraid I'm going to have to go." He started to move towards the door. "You can leave your phone number and I'll call you when I get back."

With that, he shepherded Andrew and Jess out of the door and locked up. Andrew gave him his card with his phone number and the young officer stuffed it in a pocket.

As PC Evans, drove away in a police Range Rover, Andrew and Jess started walking back over the city square and stopped in the shelter of a tree.

"What are we going to do now?" asked Jess.

"Give me a second to think," Andrew replied, pulling his collar up against the wind and rain.

-o-o-o-

The phone rang and Dan picked it up.

"Geddes Outdoor Sports," he said. "How can I help you?"

"Dan?" It sounded like Bethan's voice with a howling wind behind her. But surely she was out on the boat?

"Yes? Is that you Bethan?"

"Yes, thank God I've got hold of you Dan. The boat has lost power. And the radio's on the blink as well. Bez thinks it's been deliberately sabotaged, but I can't see anything obvious." She was speaking quickly and Dan could only just hear her words because of the noise in the background. "Anyway we're only just off the mainland which is why I thought of trying my phone. Can you call the coastguard or the lifeboat station? As I said we've got no power and we're drifting out to sea."

"Yes, sure. Whereabouts are you?"

"Just north of ..." Her words were taken by the wind.

"Say that again," Dan said loudly.

"We're just north of Ramsey Island," Bethan shouted. "Maybe a mile out to sea now. We've been drifting for about forty-five minutes while we've been trying to fix the engine."

"Okay."

"And hurry please, Dan. If the weather forecast was right the storm will be here in the next couple of hours. The wind's picking up already and we don't want to be out at sea with no power if it gets any – "

The line suddenly went dead and at the same moment the lights in the office went out and the computer screen went black. Dan looked out of the window. He couldn't see any other houses from where he was sitting. The tree in the garden was being blown back and forth by the wind and the rain was beating against the glass harder than ever.

"Bethan?" he said into the silent phone, but was no use.

He put the phone back in its cradle and picked it up again. It was still dead.

He walked quickly through to the kitchen. There was no electricity there either.

Dan went to the front door and looked out at the other houses nearby to see if they had power. He couldn't see any lights, but it was the middle of the day so maybe nobody had their lights on. And he could hardly see the houses anyway because of the driving rain.

He closed the front door again. He wished he had a mobile phone, but he had long ago decided that it was too risky.

Dan considered his options. He could go next door and see if he could use their phone, but his guess was that the electricity was out for the whole of St Davids. It was too much of a coincidence for it to just be Alun House that was without power. The storm must have brought down a electricity line somewhere.

He needed to get to the lifeboat station, but how was he going to do that?

He had his bike but that would take too long, especially in this weather.

Then he remembered that the second minibus should be parked at the back of the house. He ran to the lounge at the back of the building and looked out. It was there. A white Ford Transit minibus. He glanced at the tyres. It looked like they had been fixed after the incident a couple of days ago. So where did Bethan keep the keys?

Dan ran back to the office. There was a small cupboard on the wall, which was fortunately unlocked.

There were a few keys inside and one had the Ford logo stamped on it. He grabbed it, ran out of the front door and round to the back of the building.

By the time he reached the minibus he was soaked through. It was as if someone was throwing buckets of water at him from above. He heard thunder in the distance – the storm was coming.

He put the key in the door lock and breathed a sigh of relief as the key slid in and opened the door.

Dan started the engine and set off up the drive, wheels spinning.

As he drove through St Davids he considered stopping to see if anybody had power. He glanced at the shops but there were no lights. They looked strangely quiet. He was sure they didn't have electricity.

As Dan drove through the square in the centre of the small city, he saw the woman who had come to the office earlier. He couldn't see her face, but recognised the coat. She was standing next to a man who also had his face turned away from the driving rain. They were standing beneath a tree which wasn't giving them much shelter.

Poor couple, he thought. What a time to pick for a romantic weekend away.

As he drove away, he caught a glimpse of the profile of the man's face in the rear view mirror and had a slight feeling of familiarity, but then he had to concentrate on finding the correct road out of St Davids. He didn't want to take the wrong route and lose valuable time.

-o-o-o-

"I think we'll just have to watch Cullen until they're able to arrest him," said Andrew as they stood in the middle of the square in the pouring rain.

"Can't we just arrest him ourselves?" asked Jess. "I only worked in the admin team in Newcastle, but I'm sure members of the public can arrest someone."

"Legally any citizen has pretty much the same power of arrest as a police officer. Of course you must use proportionate force and obviously the person must have committed a crime or you leave yourself open to charges of kidnap or unlawful restraint. But the question is: where would we put him if we arrested him? We can't just tie him up for two hours. I asked him to come along peacefully last time, but unsurprisingly he declined." Andrew nodded in the direction of the building they had just left. "We need to take him to a cell and young PC Evans has just closed up the police station. I think our best course of action is to find somewhere near the Geddes Outdoor Sports building and keep an eye on him."

Andrew heard a vehicle approaching the square while he was talking and he turned round just as it went past. He caught a fleeting glimpse of the driver and then saw the words Geddes Outdoor Sports painted on the side of the minibus as it drove out of the square.

"Was that him?" Andrew wondered out loud, staring after the vehicle as it drove away down one of the roads off the square and turned a corner at the end.

"I didn't see him," replied Jess, shaking her head.

"It had Geddes Outdoor Sports written on the side," said Andrew. "You said there was only one person in the building. It must have been him."

"We could go back to their office and check?" suggested Jess.

Andrew turned to her and spoke quickly. "Right, you go and check. I'm going to get the car and follow the minibus. Ring me if you see him. Actually ring me either way."

He set off at a run towards the hotel.

-o-o-o-

Dan drove the minibus as quickly as he could down the twisting country lanes towards the lifeboat station. There were only a couple of junctions where he needed to make a choice but he was fairly sure he remembered the right way at each point.

He went over a rise and saw the three low gnarly hills that he had seen the other day. He drove past the large areas of bull rushes and reeds.

He relaxed slightly knowing that he must be on the right road and suddenly the profile of the man in the square in St Davids popped into his mind again and he thought he knew who it was. Andrew Muir. Surely not? he thought. It had only been a fleeting glimpse in the mirror and the man's hood had been up. Maybe he was seeing things. Although the woman who had been standing next to him was the person who had come to the office at Alun House – and he had thought there was something slightly strange about the conversation. Two suspicions equals a probability, he decided.

He had to leave St Davids. Better safe than sorry. He decided he would make sure the lifeboat was on its way to help Bethan's boat and then he would drive the minibus to the nearest train station and leave for another part of the country.

Despite the windscreen wipers flashing across the glass in front of him at double speed the visibility was still poor, but he drove as fast as he dared.

-o-o-o-

Jess ran quickly up to the entrance to the Geddes place, wondering if she would ever get out of this rain.

At the top of the driveway she looked at the house. All the windows were dark and the front door was now shut. She stared hard at the office window, but couldn't see anyone. She was sure the light had been on before.

Jess glanced around and thought it odd that no lights were on in any of the houses.

Oh to hell with it, she said to herself and decided to go down to the house.

She jogged down the driveway and rang the bell at the front door. No answer. She walked along the front of the house and looked in through the darkened window of the office. Nobody there.

Jess looked through a few other windows, but the house was silent.

She took out her phone to ring Andrew with the news, but found that she had no signal. How was she going to get in touch with Andrew?

She decided to run back to the hotel to phone him from there.

-o-o-o-

Andrew turned down the road that he had seen the Geddes Outdoor Sports minibus taking. He left the houses of St Davids behind and accelerated down the single track road hoping that nothing was coming the other way.

Just before a rise, he reached a fork and took what he considered to be the largest road, hoping it was the right way. At the top of the rise a flat piece of countryside stretched away in front of him. He continued driving quickly while scanning the land around him.

There, he thought. A white vehicle had appeared momentarily a mile or two ahead, directly in front of him. It had come out from behind a low rocky bluff and immediately disappeared over another rise.

Through the driving rain Andrew thought he could make out the sea in the distance.

-o-o-o-

Dan arrived at the small car park and saw the other Geddes minibus there along with a number of other cars. He parked the minibus quickly and ran down the wet steps as fast as he could.

Despite all the parked cars, he couldn't see anyone as he approached the lifeboat station.

Dan threw open the door, ran inside, wiped the rainwater from his eyes and looked around. He was surprised to see a huge space where the lifeboat should have been. The huge gates at the far end were wide open, the lifeboat ramp stretching down to the choppy waters.

Then he looked up and saw a figure in the control room above the lifeboat gateway at the far end, looking out over Ramsey Sound.

He ran up the narrow wooden steps to the control room and charged in.

"Hello," said Dan, slightly out of breath. Then he saw that the man was Geraint, the lifeboat coxswain that he'd been introduced to a few days beforehand.

"Yes?" said Geraint, turning round.

"Bethan is in trouble," said Dan. "Bethan Geddes."

"Yes? Where?"

"She took a group out on a boat trip this morning and she just phoned me and said that they've lost power and are drifting out to sea. She asked me to get the lifeboat out."

"The lifeboat went out an hour ago to help a fishing vessel that's in trouble."

Dan was confused. "Why are you here then? Why aren't you out on the lifeboat?"

"We have four coxswains and one of the other men went out today. I'm manning the station for when they come back in." Geraint calmly put up a hand. "Now stop asking questions and let me think."

For what seemed like an age, the man stood still and considered his options.

Then Geraint looked at him. "You say she phoned you? Is she near land?"

"Yes, her radio was broken but she was able to phone me. But she got cut off halfway through the call because the electricity went in St Davids."

"Yes, here too. Apparently a tree brought down the lines. The phones are down but we've got radio on battery power. Did Bethan say where she was?"

"Just north of Ramsey Island about a mile out to sea."

"How many people on board?"

"Her and Bez plus about eight customers."

"She's in the Treginnis?"

"What's that?" asked Dan.

"That's the name of her rigid hull inflatable boat. Twin engined, can carry a dozen people."

"I suppose so. She didn't say."

"Must be then."

Geraint held up his hand and Dan waited for him to think again.

"Right." Geraint announced. "We've got an inshore lifeboat that takes a crew of two or three in the old station back there." He pointed to the back of the building. "It's a small rigid hull inflatable which isn't really intended for going out in seas like this, but maybe we should be able to tow the Treginnis back if she hasn't gone too far out. And you're going to come with me."

"Me?" said Dan in amazement.

"Yes, I can't do it on my own. And first I'm going to the house half a mile back up the road. A man called Owen lives there and I'll ask him to fetch someone to man the station. Ciaran."

"You mean Ciaran who works for Bethan? But he phoned in sick this morning."

"I know. I spoke to him earlier, but he can be ill here."

Dan just shrugged.

"Come with me," said Geraint and they walked back down the narrow wooden steps into the main hall. He led Dan to a row of pegs on the wall, some of which held bright yellow all-in-one waterproof overalls.

"Get yourself into one of these," the coxswain said, "but not mine." He pointed to a peg which said Geraint at the top. "And some boots and a buoyancy aid." Each set of overalls had some boots standing on the floor beneath them and the buoyancy aids were hanging up a little further down the wall. "And put your valuables, car keys and so on in that box there."

With that, Geraint left the building.

Dan stood there for a second. He needed to leave the area quickly – if the person in St Davids really had been Andrew Muir. But Geraint said he needed him to help. Dan agonised over his decision.

Then he shrugged his shoulders and decided to do as Geraint had instructed him.

He took some overalls and started climbing into them. He realised they were going to be a little tight and grabbed some that looked larger.

Dan tugged the overalls over his legs, pushed his arms in and heaved the garment over his shoulders. Even the larger size was a tight fit and it took him a while to pull them on. He looked through the boots until he found some the right size, sat on the bottom of the steps to the control room and pulled them on. He stood up, walked over to the buoyancy aids, put one on and tightened the straps.

Dan looked at his watch. It must have taken him five or ten minutes to get the clothes on. He thought he'd have to practice if he was ever going to be part of a lifeboat crew.

He started walking towards the door and heard footsteps outside. Geraint's back already, he thought, that was quick.

The door at the back of the building opened slowly and, to his horror, he realised it was Andrew Muir stepping through.

Dan looked behind him, but the only escape route was down the lifeboat ramp. And now was not the time to dive into the sea, he realised. He was wearing a life jacket but he wouldn't get very far. And in any case, he needed to help Geraint.

He turned back to see Muir smiling at him.

"Hello, Mr Cullen," Andrew said. "I thought we would meet again."

"And I was hoping you might have given up."

Andrew laughed. "I don't suppose you'd care to accompany me back to the police station, would you Mr Cullen?"

"How did you find me this time?"

"I'll always find you."

"But how on earth did you know I was in St Davids?" Dan asked. "Did I make another mistake?" He shook his head and looked at the floor, thinking back through everything he had done. "Nobody knew I was in St Davids and I've only been here a couple of days."

"If it's any consolation I nearly got you in London at the beginning of the week, but you just wriggled through my fingers. It was a clever trick leaving by coach when you'd arrived by train."

Dan was astonished that Andrew knew so much about his movements. And then he realised. "You know about Sophie."

Andrew regretted mentioning London now. He shouldn't have let Cullen know that they were keeping Sophie under surveillance. Why had he been so stupid? It had just been showing off, wanting Cullen to know that he was cleverer than him.

At that moment, the door opened and Geraint came back in.

He registered Andrew's presence but just headed for the overalls. "Can I help you?" Geraint said to Andrew.

"That's okay," replied Muir. "I'm just here to take this man away."

"You can't take him away now," said Geraint and started putting on his bright yellow overalls. "I need him."

"This man is an escaped criminal and I'm going to take him away."

Geraint glanced at Dan as he did up the front of his overalls and then looked back at Andrew. "He doesn't seem like a criminal to me. He's about to risk his life to save others."

Andrew was confused. "What are you talking about?"

"Our main lifeboat has gone out to help a trawler that's in trouble." Geraint pulled on his boots. "But there's another vessel that needs help. A small boat with ten people on board has lost power. We have a small inshore lifeboat that I can't crew alone if I'm going to have any chance of helping these people and I need Dan here to help me."

"You're not taking this man away from me," said Andrew. "I've been chasing him for a long time and there's no way I'm letting him out of my sight."

"You can come with us," said Geraint, pulling on his buoyancy aid and clipping it up. "Another pair of hands wouldn't hurt."

"What?" said Andrew.

Geraint walked over and stood in front of Andrew. "Our inshore lifeboat takes a crew of two or three. I'm not going out alone. I intend to help these people but we have to move fast. There's a big storm coming and this boat isn't built for big waves. We need to get out there and get back quickly. And you need to make a decision right now – if you want to help me then put on a set of those overalls, a pair of boots and a buoyancy aid. Dan and I are going to get the boat out."

Geraint turned and walked to the door. Dan smiled at Andrew and followed the coxswain.

Andrew stood for a moment looking at the door as it closed behind them. Then he shrugged and lifted a set of overalls from a peg.

20. All At Sea. St Justinians. Saturday Afternoon.

Geraint and Dan walked to the old lifeboat station that was behind the new building, set into a recess in the hillside. The coxswain unlocked the gates to the old wooden shed and pulled them wide, unveiling a small, red, inflatable boat on a trailer. He took a rope from the wall of the building and threw it in the boat.

Geraint fetched a triangular device from the back of the shed and put that in as well. He saw Dan looking at it and said: "Bridle."

"Bridle?" said Dan.

"For towing. Keeps the rope away from the propeller."

Dan nodded as Geraint went round to the front of the small lifeboat.

"Grab the back end," Geraint said. Dan did as he was told.

Geraint pulled the boat out of the shed with Dan pushing from the other end. They guided it down the slipway and into the water. The coxswain unfastened the boat from the trailer and floated it off. He passed the rope to Dan and told him to hold the boat in place.

Geraint took the trailer back up the old lifeboat station.

As he was walking back down the slipway, Andrew appeared dressed in the same protective clothing as the others.

Geraint looked at him. "Did you take those overalls off a peg marked Bronwyn?"

"I think so."

"Do you know that Bronwyn is a girl's name? Those overalls are a little small for you."

"I just presumed they were meant to be tight," said Andrew, holding out his arms and looking down at himself.

"Well there's no time to change. Let's go." Geraint turned towards the boat and took the rope from Dan. "You two get in."

Dan and Andrew clambered into the inflatable and then Geraint jumped in after them. He moved to the back of the boat and started the engines.

Geraint smoothly reversed the lifeboat away from the slipway and then set it going forwards. The boat accelerated quickly until it was skipping across the tops of the waves.

"What's your name?" Geraint shouted.

"Andrew," Muir called back to him while holding tightly to the sides of the boat as it bounced across the water.

"I'm Geraint."

The coxswain directed the lifeboat towards the northern end of Ramsey Island and in less than a minute they were past it and out in the open sea.

The waves were higher out here and the rain was still lashing down. Dan was warm enough inside his overalls but his face was already icy cold from the wind and the water that was splashing up from the sea and falling from the sky. He hardly noticed it though. All of his attention was focussed on the waves that towered around the small inflatable. Dan felt like he was on a roller coaster as the boat slid down into a trough and then raced up to the next peak.

"Keep your eyes peeled," shouted Geraint about the noise of wind and the boat's twin engines.

Dan and Andrew had been concentrating solely on holding on to the boat but now they raised their eyes to look around for the Treginnis. The sky was very dark although it was only mid-afternoon and they were only able to see more than a few yards when they were perched on the crest of a wave.

Whenever their boat reached the top of a swell, the three men looked around quickly in all directions. The sheets of rain reduced their visibility immensely and Dan realised this was going to be a difficult job.

"Don't you know where they are?" bellowed Andrew.

"We know they were a mile offshore just north of Ramsey Island," replied Geraint. "How long ago was that Dan?"

"Maybe forty-five minutes," shouted Dan, glancing at his watch.

"The current should be taking them north-west," said Geraint. "I'm going to go out a couple of miles, turn north for a while and then head back in. And then we'll repeat the process heading north each time until we find them."

"How long can we stay out here?" shouted Andrew.

"We've got enough fuel for three hours at maximum speed. Should be plenty."

For the next twenty minutes Geraint criss-crossed the ocean and they all peered into the gloom as the rain beat down on their faces. Dan found the raindrops mesmerising and the rolling of the boat across the sea added to the sensation.

"They've gone further than I expected," shouted Geraint.

"What's that over there?" cried Andrew suddenly, pointing to starboard. Dan looked just as a red shape dropped out of view.

Geraint turned to head towards it. At the top of the next wave they looked again, but didn't see anything. Then on the next crest, they saw it once more. It was definitely a large, red, inflatable – and then it vanished into another trough.

"That's it," shouted Geraint.

They steadily closed the distance between the two boats and soon they were able to recognise the shapes of Bethan and Bez standing at the stern. The two of them had now spotted the lifeboat and they were waving furiously.

Geraint covered the last few hundred yards quickly and then slowed to pull alongside the Treginnis. Bez leaned over and grabbed hold of the rope that ran around the edge of the lifeboat and Andrew and Dan did the same on their boat. They held on tight as the sea took them up and down together.

"Would you like a tow?" shouted Geraint in his usual under-stated fashion.

"Thank God you're here," said Bethan. There were a lot of relieved faces on the people sitting in the boat. The young girl, Asha, hugged her father. "Why are you in Myrtle though?" Bethan asked.

"Garside was called out." Geraint set up the bridle and the rope while Dan and Andrew held the boats together. Geraint threw the other end of the rope over to Bez who threaded it a couple of times through a loop on the front of the Treginnis, but did not tie it away.

"You hold tight to that Bez," Geraint shouted over to him, "but let it go if there's a problem. You know the drill. I'll come back for you."

"Okay."

"And remember you want to be one wave length back."

Without any further discussion, Geraint slowly set off back in the direction of Ramsey Sound. The rope played out and then went tight. Geraint steadily increased the speed and soon they were making decent progress.

"We're a fair way up the coast now, aren't we?" shouted Dan. "How long do you think until we get back?"

"Thirty minutes or so," he replied. "You keep an eye on the Treginnis for me and shout if it's getting too close."

There was a flash of lightening followed by a crack of thunder a couple of seconds later and Dan realised they were nearly in the middle of the storm now. He had thought the waves were big when they set off, but they were twice the size now.

Geraint seemed to be working hard, making sure they approached each swell correctly considering both their own boat and the one behind.

"Can I do anything?" yelled Dan.

Geraint shook his head, not taking his eyes off the next wave.

They made steady progress over the next twenty minutes and occasionally glimpsed land off to their left. It all looked the same to Dan, but he could see Geraint study the features of the land for a moment each time and nod to himself. He hoped the older man knew where he was.

Eventually Dan could see more land looming out of the gloom ahead of them. Then another flash of lightening illuminated the world around them for a second and Dan saw that it was Ramsey Island ahead.

"Now comes the tricky part," shouted Geraint.

"So it hasn't been tricky up to now?" yelled Andrew.

"As we approach land the waves will start to break and we don't want one of them coming down on top of us. We should be okay if we can make it into the sound – the water there should be a little calmer."

Geraint aimed at the midpoint between the island and the mainland, but he also had to maintain the right approach to each wave – and these were getting progressively bigger and more white-topped.

Dan looked back again at the Treginnis and saw to his horror that a huge wave was right behind the larger boat, looking like it was about to break. "Bez, look out!" he shouted. Bez had already seen the wave though and was shouting at the people in his boat to hold on.

Geraint glanced back, saw what was happening and accelerated as fast as he could in an attempt to move the Treginnis out of harm's way. The larger boat picked up speed but then effectively caught the big wave like a surfer. Geraint glanced back again. The Treginnis was catching them.

"Release!" Geraint shouted back to Bez. The younger man instantly let go of the rope holding the two boats together and Geraint quickly turned the smaller inflatable out of the path of the oncoming larger boat just in time.

The Treginnis ran forward under the power of the wave in the direction of Ramsey Island, but just as quickly as it had appeared the wave melted away again. Unfortunately the larger boat was now in the area where other waves were breaking as they approached the northern end of the island.

Geraint gritted his teeth and headed for the Treginnis in order to set up the tow rope again. The small lifeboat was buffeted from side to side and water poured into the boat and then out again. Dan and Andrew hung on to stop themselves being washed overboard. Geraint sat immovable at the tiller.

Waves kept pushing the Treginnis nearer and nearer to Ramsey Island and each time they were almost alongside another surge of water pushed them apart again.

Then Dan heard Andrew shout: "Oh no!" He turned and saw what Andrew was looking at: an immense wave just at their stern. It towered over them like the side of a house.

Geraint started to shout: "Make for the island if – "

And that was the last Dan heard, because the wave chose that moment to crash down on top of them. It was like being hit by a truck and then he was tumbling out of the boat and into the sea, under the water, swirling around until he didn't know which way was up.

He felt like he was under water for hours, but finally he burst up above the surface. The life jacket had done all of the work for him - he had been helpless against the absolute power of the sea. As soon as his head was above water, he managed to suck in a mouthful of air before a wave crashed over him again.

Fortunately this wave was smaller than the previous one and he wasn't under for as long this time. When he re-surfaced he felt a powerful hand seize the back of his buoyancy aid. He looked around and saw Bez – and it was like looking up into the face of an angel.

Bez was leaning far out of the boat – he later learned that one of the men was holding on to his legs – and he pulled Dan towards him.

"Grab hold of the boat," Bez shouted at him. "I can't lift you in."

Dan turned and clutched the rope that ran around the side of the inflatable. He glanced over and saw that Andrew was holding onto the side of the boat as well, but there was no sign of Geraint.

"Hold tight mate," shouted Bez, pulling himself back into the boat. "We're heading for land."

Dan looked in the direction Bez had been looking and saw that they were only a hundred yards from the island. This isn't good, he thought to himself. He didn't think there had been any beaches on Ramsey Island when he had been looking at it the other day. It was either cliffs rising vertically out of the sea or at best it was land sloping steeply at more than forty-five degrees – and there would surely be rocks at the bottom of those slopes.

A wave pushed the Treginnis another twenty yards on before rushing past them to crash against the island – and then another and another. Then, through the spray and the waves, Dan thought he saw an inlet carved into the side of a steep hillside. It looked like they were being pushed into there – to be battered against the inlet walls no doubt.

The next wave broke just behind them and hurtled the boat into the narrow inlet at breakneck speed. And then to Dan's relief he saw that the small inlet opened out again to a width of about fifty yards.

The widening of the waterway was just enough to slow their rate of travel to a still brisk but un-threatening pace and the wave surged forward to deposit them on a beach of shingle at the innermost end of the inlet.

Dan was still clutching onto the side of the boat and his knees were dragged over the stones before the wave subsided back past him. He lay there for a moment, the lower part of his body on the rounded pebbles, his hands still gripping the rope on the side of the boat. Although he must only have been in the water for less than sixty seconds he was exhausted.

"Get up, Dan," shouted Bez, just as the next wave crashed over his shoulders.

Bethan was getting the passengers out of the other side of the boat and up the shingle beach. Andrew was scrambling up the stones to join them. Bez pulled at the back of Dan's buoyancy aid trying to encourage him to stand up. When then water subsided again, Dan got weakly to his feet just before the next wave crashed against his legs.

He staggered a little and then used the rope on the side of the boat to pull himself up the sloping beach, while Bez supported him.

They walked up to the top of the shingles, out of reach of the water, and slumped down next to the rest of the group.

"Where's Geraint?" asked Dan. His only answer was a flash of lightening followed immediately by a boom of thunder that echoed around the small inlet.

21. Fish Out Of Water. Ramsey Island. Saturday Evening.

"Geraint will be alright," said Bez. "He's indestructible." The tone of his voice didn't sound as sure as his words.

Suddenly Bethan pointed at the water. "What's that?" she shouted.

At the mouth of the inlet, being carried forward by a wave, was a bright yellow object with a flash of red. As it was brought nearer they realised that it was a limp human figure with its face in the water.

"It must be Geraint," shouted Bez and he ran down to the water and dived in. A huge wave pushed him back momentarily, but he forced his way forward again and started swimming out, ducking through the waves. At the same time Geraint was carried towards him and, as they came together, Bez was able to grab hold of the man's red buoyancy aid.

He half-pulled and half-surfed Geraint's body to the shore and, with Bethan's help, dragged him up the shingle. They turned him onto his back and Bez checked his airway and began performing compressions on his chest.

Almost immediately, seawater spluttered out of his mouth and Geraint started coughing. Bez helped him sit up.

"I told you he was indestructible," Bez said, looking up at Bethan.

They let Geraint recover his breath and then helped him up to where the others were sitting. Fortunately they had found a place where the small cliff formed an overhang above them and they were sheltered from the wind and the worst of the rain. They sat Geraint down on the pebbles, leaning against a large rock. He continued to cough up more water, but at least he was moving.

"Is anyone else hurt?" asked Bethan looking at the rest of her group.

"I think my daughter might have broken her arm," said Radeep Addison, the man who Dan remembered had arrived late at the office that morning. He was hugging his daughter, who was sobbing quietly and holding her arm. "I think she got banged against the seat in front when one of those waves came over us."

"We have a sling in the first aid kit in the boat – I'll see if it's still there," Bethan said. She walked quickly down to the boat and came back up with the kit.

"Can I have a look at your arm, please?" Bethan said to the girl. "I'm not a doctor, but I've done a little bit of first aid."

Bethan examined the girl's arm, trying to move it as little as possible.

"I can't tell if it's broken," Bethan said. "Hopefully that's a good sign – if I can't tell it's broken then it shouldn't be too bad."

She put the sling in place, supporting the girl's arm.

"You're being very brave," she said to the girl. "I'd be screaming if it was me."

The girl smiled weakly.

"Your name is Asha, isn't it?" Bethan said as she finished off the sling.

The girl nodded.

"I'm sorry the trip hasn't turned out as we planned."

"That's okay," Asha said bravely.

"This was her birthday present," her father, Radeep, said. "It was her birthday last weekend and we gave her the ticket for this trip as a present. She's always loved seals and dolphins."

"I'm so sorry," said Bethan. "We'll try and make it up to you." She turned to Asha. "We'll give you a trip every year on your birthday – if you want. But we'll only go out when it's beautiful sunshine."

The girl smiled and nodded.

"At least we're safely on land now and somebody should be able to get us off the island soon," Bethan said.

"Has anyone seen the lifeboat?" It was Geraint. He started getting to his feet.

"Sit down, Geraint," said Bethan. "I thought we'd lost you earlier and I don't want you keeling over."

"I'm okay. What about the lifeboat?"

"I saw you three come out of it," Bez said, "and it shot off in front of the wave. I think it'll be down the other end of the sound by now."

"Have you got any flares in the Treginnis?" Geraint asked.

"We did have, but I used them earlier," Bethan replied. "Not that it did much good."

"And the radio is broken?"

"Yes."

"Does anyone have a mobile phone with signal?" Geraint asked of the group.

There was a rustling and shuffling as everybody unzipped their waterproof overalls and got out their phones. One by one, they shook their heads.

"I've got plenty of power," said Bez. "But zero signal."

"Electricity must still be out on the mainland." Geraint looked up at the sky. "We need to get to the east side of the island and signal to the lifeboat station somehow before it gets dark. We've probably got a couple of hours."

"You're not going anywhere, Geraint," said Bethan.

"I'm okay. Don't worry about me."

"I'll go," said Dan.

"And me," said Bez.

"All three of us will go," said Geraint. "Would you mind looking after your people, Bethan? I think this is as good a place as any to shelter for now and we don't want to move Asha until we have to."

"Are there no buildings on the island?" Dan asked.

"Not any more. People used to live here, but the buildings are just ruins now – no better than the shelter we've got here."

Geraint looked around. The inlet continued to narrow at the top of the beach. Where the two low cliffs came together, there was a jumble of rocks and it looked like they would be able to climb up to the land above them.

"We'll head up there," Geraint said. He turned to Bethan. "We'll come back shortly after dark at the latest. If we're going to spend the night it might as well be down here rather than up there in the wind and rain."

"I hope you can make contact with someone," Bethan replied. "It'll be cold here if we have to stay the night. And we don't have any food of course. And poor old Asha's arm."

Geraint squeezed her shoulder. "We'll do our best."

He turned and set off. Dan and Bez followed him. Dan marvelled at the man's constitution.

A second later Andrew, who had been quiet all this time, fell in behind them as well.

Geraint glanced back, saw Andrew but simply faced forwards again and continued walking up the beach.

Bez followed Geraint's look and realised Andrew was coming with them. "Er, who are you?" Bez asked, as though seeing Andrew for the first time.

"Andrew Muir. Pleased to meet you." He held out his hand.

Bez shook hands, his face expressing his confusion. "I'm Bez. But how is it that you're here exactly? You're not on the lifeboat team."

"I'm with this guy," Andrew replied, indicating Dan. "Where he goes, I go."

Bez opened his mouth to say something, but then noticed that Geraint was moving away from them. Bez shrugged and decided to leave further questions for later.

The four men clambered up the rocks and onto the grasslands above. The wind once again became a howling gale and the rain was still coming down hard.

Geraint and Bez peered through the gloom in the direction of where they thought the mainland should be and then set off. Dan and Andrew followed behind.

They walked around the north-eastern edge of the small island for about twenty minutes. For most of its coastline the island was high above the level of the sea. They passed a small, tumble-down building with dry stone walls of slate. The roof had long since disappeared and the old ruin was simply a shell. Dan wondered if people had lived there or if it had been a barn. Just past the building they reached a small promontory which stretched a hundred yards into the sound and Geraint led them to the end and looked out across the water.

"The lifeboat station is over there," the older man shouted above the roar of the wind.

Dan stared into the gathering darkness, blinking as the raindrops hit his face, and all he could see was the shadowy outline of the land. As the rain ebbed and flowed, he thought that he caught glimpses of the white walls of the lifeboat building, but he couldn't be sure.

"I'll have to take your word for it," replied Andrew, turning away.

Bez started waving. "You never know, they might be looking out for us," he said.

"I can't believe that they'll see us, I'm afraid," Andrew said. "We can barely see the lifeboat station and it's fifty feet high."

Bez dropped his arms. "Can we signal with anything?" he said, looking around.

Nobody answered. There was nothing. The island had no trees so there was no wood for building a fire, even if it had been possible in this deluge.

Geraint had been standing looking into the rain. "I think the boat's back in the station."

"How can you tell?" Bez said, staring across the water. Dan just shook his head.

"I think the gates are closed. Occasionally the visibility improves for a second and you can just make the building out."

"If only we could let them know we're here," said Bez. "They could just pop over and get us. It's so annoying – they're only a few hundred yards away."

"I think that all we can do is wait here for a break in the weather and then signal to them," said Geraint. "I can't think of another option."

"We have to hope it's in the next hour and a half, before it gets too dark."

Geraint turned back to Dan and Andrew. "There's no point all of us being out here in the cold. Why don't you two head back to that old building and shelter there for a while."

"No, we'll wait here with you," said Dan.

"Go on," said Geraint. "You can come back and take our place in half an hour."

Dan realised that this was probably the sensible option. They were still wearing their bright yellow suits which protected them from the wind to a certain extent, but they were wet through.

Dan nodded. "Okay, we'll be back in thirty minutes."

He and Andrew turned away and trudged back to the small, run-down building. Two of the walls were just waist high, but the other two were still their original height.

They went in and Dan sat down on the floor in the corner made by the two good walls. Andrew sat down next to him.

"It's a bit better in here," said Dan.

"Aye, a bit," admitted Andrew.

They sat in silence for a few minutes.

"Was it the postcard or the telephone calls?" asked Dan after a while. "Or both?"

Andrew gave a short laugh. "What postcard?" he said.

"So it *was* the postcard then."

"It doesn't matter what it was this time. I know everything about you and you were bound to make a mistake sooner or later."

"I know a little about you as well now, you know," Dan said.

Andrew didn't respond.

"After meeting you in Cornwall last year, I wanted to find out about my adversary. Know your enemy," Dan said. "You were born thirty six years ago at the Royal Alexandra Hospital in Paisley near Glasgow. Your birthday is on the October 2nd just a few days before mine, which makes us both Libra."

"I don't believe in that rubbish."

"Neither do I. But it's interesting that we were born a few days apart, don't you think?"

"No, it's just coincidence."

"Anyway, you grew up in a small village called Balloch near Loch Lomond and then moved down to Manchester when you were ten years old. Your father was Quality Assurance Manager for Jopp Engineering but had to move when they merged with another company."

"Am I on *This Is Your Life*?"

"You did fairly well at school, but only got a B and two C's for your A Levels, which you were probably a little disappointed with." Dan glanced at Andrew, but got no reaction. "But it was enough to get you onto a Forensic Psychology degree at the University of Liverpool where you got a first. You joined DHC straight from university where you're now setting up the Personal Injury Claim Unit for the insurance arm of ZBS."

That got a reaction from Andrew. "How do you know that?" he said sharply. "We've only been working on that for a few weeks."

"Your home address," Dan continued, "is 22 Morrice Road, Twickenham – a small terraced house. You could have afforded a bigger place but it wouldn't have sat well with your Presbyterian upbringing."

"You don't know anything about me."

"I didn't before, but I know a little now. My main concern is that you don't have any hobbies or interests. You used to play football when you were young. Apparently you were pretty good, but you haven't played since university. And you don't have any other interests, which is a real shame because that means you're as obsessed with your job as I feared."

"I like gardening," Andrew smiled.

"It didn't look like it."

That also got a reaction. "You haven't seen my house," Andrew insisted, but knew in his heart that Dan had been there.

"I came to London to see a friend in November and decided to stay and watch you for a few days. You just went to work, came home, went for a run and then read a book or worked. You don't even have a television."

Andrew was quiet for a few moments. "Everything's rubbish on television these days," he said in the end. "But you're right about one thing. I am obsessed. I'm obsessed with doing a good job and catching people like you."

"I think we're quite alike you know," Dan said. "I like to think that if things had happened differently that we might have been friends."

"I'm nothing like you."

"We both want justice."

"But you're prepared to steal for it. Where would we be if everyone dispensed their own justice?"

"So it's okay for you to mete out justice but not me?"

"All I do is track people down and hand them over for others to work that out," argued Andrew. "Our society has devised a process for assessing justice over thousands of years, a system that has checks and balances so that it is as fair as possible to all parties. I'm helping that process and you're undermining it."

"Do you think it's fair for a person to be ill when help is available?" asked Dan.

"You might as well ask if I think taxes should be doubled or trebled. You can't spend an infinite amount of money on the health service."

"So you think that a certain type of illness should go untreated just to save money?"

"Personally I would vote for an increase in taxes," Andrew replied. "People don't need to go on three holidays a year and buy so much junk. They can afford to pass some of their money to others who need it." He looked at Dan. "Would you vote for higher taxes? Someone who worked at the heart of the capitalist system – I wouldn't have thought so."

"I used to think that capitalism was the best of a bad lot, but now I'm not so sure. Communism doesn't work though – it just results in stagnation or exploitation. It's like when you go to the restaurant in a big group and you say you're going to split the bill. Everyone thinks 'oh I might as well have a starter' or they get few more drinks. Communism – or socialism for that matter – is like that."

"You can't compare socialism to people getting extra drinks in a restaurant."

"It's the same principle. It only works if people do the right thing, but there will always be people who want to take a little more for doing slightly less. Egalitarianism only works alongside altruism."

"It's even worse with capitalism – the taking is more extreme."

"At least they work hard to do it. And it's the spirit of competition that drives the human race forwards. If there's someone right beside you in a race, it makes you run just a little faster."

"So everyone paying their own bills and fighting against each other to win the race?" Andrew asked, knowing Dan had painted himself into a corner.

"Yeah, okay, I know that's not what I've been doing," Dan replied. He paused a moment then continued: "Don't you wonder why the political parties are so similar these days? Is it because we're nearly at the right solution? For a couple of hundred years we've oscillated between parties who believe in competition or fairness, when what you want is a blend of the two. Perhaps the wavelength of the oscillation is narrowing in around the perfect midpoint though?"

"And ultimately we'll have one party? That sounds like stagnation again."

"Oh I don't know," said Dan, with a shake of his head. "I haven't worked it out yet. Perhaps we need to rip it all up and start again."

"You're starting to sound extremist now."

"Somebody needs to change the world. We can't all accept the status quo."

"You can't change the world, Cullen."

"Who are you to say I can't?" replied Dan. "I just need to work out what I'm going to change it to."

Andrew laughed.

"Why are you laughing at me?" smiled Dan, knowing he was sounding foolish. "We're both passionate about what we believe in and we both want fairness."

"And you want the world to think you're some kind of Robin Hood, stealing from the big bad banks and giving it to the poor, sick children." Andrew turned to look at Dan. "I know the first chunk of money that you stole was for your niece but we've also tracked the other nine million that you stole. And this morning, I spoke to some of the people that you gave it to. They told me you were a hero and I told them that you were a common thief."

"But they were all ill and nobody was helping them."

"Don't worry, I know all about it. I spoke to five people whose children have the same condition as your niece and they were denied treatment because of the expense. And I spoke to other people who had other rare illnesses for which there were only experimental drugs that were hugely expensive. You stole millions from ZBS and gave it to these people. You think you were doing a good thing, but you can't steal."

Dan sighed. "I was just re-distributing the wealth a little. A parent needs to show a child the right way to behave. And the world is a child." Then he shook his head. "Sorry, I didn't mean that to sound so grandiose. All I'm saying is: there are some people I want to help. And I'm not just going to drift around the country, trying to avoid you. I need to bring things to a head and solve the problem properly."

"Don't worry – the problem is solved," Andrew replied. "I've got you and you're going to prison."

Dan laughed. "You haven't got me. We're simply sitting side-by-side in a ruined old building on an island."

"As soon as we get rescued you'll be going to prison."

"That doesn't sound too bad actually," Dan sighed. "I'm getting a little tired of running around the country. I did think it would be wonderful to be free – and it has been for a while – but soon you want to settle down and sleep in the same bed each night." He looked over at Andrew. "I thought of something the other day. I thought to myself: 'I'm as free as a fish'. A fish can travel across the whole world if he wants, but in reality he's trapped by the surface of the water. I've got to swim under the surface wherever I go, making sure that people don't notice me – and fish are always on the move as well, governed more by movements in the environment around them rather than their own free will. And they never stop. It must be tiring to be a fish."

"I've heard it all before," Andrew said. "Normally they just tell me that they're tired of running – they don't come up with some complex fish analogy. Don't worry, I'll put you in a little fish tank somewhere and every day they'll feed you."

"As I said, it sounds nice," admitted Dan. "But unfortunately I've got more work to do. I haven't worked out the whole plan yet, but there are some things that I've already set in motion that I need to finish. I can't go with you yet."

With that, Dan turned onto his side and stood up. He arched his back. "I must be getting old," he said, as he stretched. "Anyway, I think we've done enough setting the world to rights there. Perhaps now isn't really the time to sit and discuss politics – do you think that we should go and see if Geraint and Bez want to have a break?"

Andrew nodded. "I think we should go and see," he agreed, starting to get up, "but it wouldn't surprise me if Geraint wanted to carry on."

They walked back out along the promontory to where the other two men were standing. The weather didn't seem to have eased at all.

"Any joy?" Dan shouted, above the noise of the wind.

Geraint shook his head.

"There hasn't been a gap in the rain at all," Bez yelled. "Occasionally we can faintly see the lifeboat station, but not clearly enough."

"It's frustrating," Dan said. "It's just over there and we've got no way of getting to them."

"I keep thinking that if only I had my kayak then I could get over there in five minutes."

"With the weather like this?" Dan asked.

"Yeah it's not too bad in the sound with the tide as it is right now. That's why they put the lifeboat station there – it's like a bay, sheltered from the open sea. And it's nearly low tide so it'd be quite safe at the moment, even with the storm."

Dan had a sudden thought. "Hang on, you said the other day that the water rushes through here at ten to fifteen miles an hour?"

"That's when the tide's coming in or going out. At low and high tide it's fairly quiet."

"Well in that case I could swim it."

"You're joking," said Bez. Geraint turned back from looking across the water to look at Dan.

"What is it, half a mile?" said Dan. "I used to do that as a warm-up when I was doing swimming training as a teenager."

"But it's different in the sea," Bez argued.

"You just said it's like a sheltered bay."

"Yeah, a sheltered bay in the middle of a raging storm."

Dan looked out at the water and then at Geraint. "How big would you say the waves are at the moment?"

"Five to ten feet in the sound."

"That's not too bad. I'm a pretty strong swimmer," said Dan. "And I'd have the buoyancy aid."

Bez and Geraint looked at each other. Dan could tell they were tempted by the idea.

"What do you think?" Bez said to the older man.

"If Dan says he can do it, then it's worth a try," Geraint replied. "We don't want to spend the night here in the rain, with no food. And that girl has a broken arm. If you're sure, Dan."

"I'm happy to do it. Half a mile isn't much. For a few years I swam a mile or two every day."

"Well let's make it a little shorter for you," Geraint said. "We'll walk down to The Bitches. The sound is half the width there."

"Is it safe there?" Dan asked in surprise.

"Yeah, it's fine at low tide," said Bez. "You could even rest on the rocks halfway across if you get tired."

"It's about an hour before full dark and also an hour before low tide," said Geraint. "You don't want to be in the middle of the sound in two or three hours time when the tide starts coming in at its fastest. How long would it take you to swim quarter of a mile?"

"Maybe 20-30 minutes in calm water. Double that perhaps in this sea."

"Well it will take us half an hour to walk down to The Bitches but that should give you enough time," Geraint said.

"What are we waiting for then?" Dan said.

Andrew had been listening to this conversation, becoming more and more agitated.

"No," he said finally. "You can't do it."

"Why not?" asked Bez.

"I'm not letting him."

"Who *are* you anyway?" said Bez.

"This man that you're calling Dan is actually called Stephen Cullen. He has stolen a large sum of money from a bank and I'm the investigator who has been assigned to track him down. Now that I've caught up with him, I'm not letting him go."

"Wow," said Bez, turning to Dan. "You really stole money from a bank?"

"Technically that might be true," Dan replied, "but – "

"Whoa, dude, you're a bank robber. How much did you get?"

"That's not important," Andrew interrupted. "The significant thing is that I don't let him out of my sight until I can get him to prison."

"Dan's offered to swim across that," Bez said, pointing at the waters raging in front of them, "so he doesn't seem like one of the bad guys to me. You could go I suppose?"

"I can't swim that," said Andrew.

"Well why don't you let someone who can? We don't want to spend the whole night here, do we? And there's no guarantee they'll get us off tomorrow. The storm is forecast to continue."

"But – ", started Andrew.

"We're wasting time," said Geraint suddenly and started walking. Dan and Bez smiled at each other and followed him.

Andrew fumed for a moment and then set off in pursuit, knowing that he was going to lose his man soon, but wanting to keep him in sight for as long as possible.

22. As Free As A Fish. Ramsey Sound. Saturday Evening.

"There they are," Bez said. He smiled at Dan. "They're not so bad at low tide."

It was now dusk, but Dan could still see the line of rocks known as The Bitches stretching out into the sound. Some were only just above the level of the water and others were quite a few feet proud of the waterline and a few metres long.

"The rocks stretch almost halfway across the sound," said Geraint. He was still having to talk loudly to be heard above the roar of the wind and the rain was still falling heavily. "The best plan might be to climb along them for as long as possible until you have to swim. There will be some gaps along the way but you can jump into the water and climb out again."

"The rocks look pretty rough," Dan said.

"They're not too bad," replied Bez. "You wouldn't want to hit them in a boat, but they should be okay to climb along if you keep your shoes on. Whatever you think is best though, Dan."

"It's probably a good idea, it'll be tiring enough just swimming a few hundred yards in this weather."

"The wind's coming from the north, so the waves are hitting this side of the rocks. Try and stay the other side as you clamber along."

Dan had decided to take off the yellow waterproof overalls that he'd been wearing, but keep his underwear and t-shirt for when he was on the other side. He disrobed quickly and put the slimline buoyancy aid back on. He tied his shoes as tight as possible so they wouldn't get pulled off in the sea.

Standing there in just his t-shirt, he shivered with the cold. "No point hanging around," he said and waded out to the first rock.

"Tell them to come to this part of the island," shouted Geraint. "This little bay here is known as Ramsey harbour. They'll know where you mean."

"Okay," Dan shouted over his shoulder and climbed up the rock. It was covered with seaweed which made the going difficult. He held onto the top of the rock while he edged sideways along it.

When he got to the end of that rock there was a gap of three or four metres to the next rock. The water seemed to be travelling quickly through the gap, especially when a wave crashed through it.

Dan put his foot in the water to test whether he could wade across. It didn't seem too deep but it was freezing cold.

He waited until a wave had just passed and started wading through the gap. He quickly sank to waist deep, but fortunately no further. He found it difficult to keep his balance, but pushed forward as quickly as he could. Just before the next wave came through the gap he managed to get into the shelter of the next rock. He climbed onto it and edged along it.

The next gap was a little wider. Once again he waited until a wave had just past and then waded out. Within a couple of feet he was waist deep again and then on his next step the floor just disappeared. He lost his footing and sank beneath the freezing water. He burst up again, breathing hard, partly due to the cold and partly due to the shock. He saw that he had been washed a few feet away from the line of rocks, but fortunately he had been taken into the still water behind the rock he had been heading for.

Dan swam the couple of strokes back to the rock and breathed a sigh of relief when his foot touched something solid under the water. He climbed up onto the rock and rested for a second.

"Are you okay?" shouted Bez. He was only thirty yards away but Dan could only just hear him above the wind. Dan raised a hand in acknowledgement.

He moved along the slippery seaweed and then saw that, although there was only a small gap to the next rock, it was only just above the level of the water. Waves were pouring over the rock submerging it completely for a couple of seconds. And with the size of the waves he didn't think he would be able to stop himself from being pushed into the sea.

He decided on his course of action.

As soon as a wave had gone past, he jumped across the small gap onto the rock, slipped onto one knee jarring it hard, stood up again, ran forward as best he could on the seaweed and jumped into the next gap.

A wave caught him just as he was re-surfacing and pushed him a few yards away from the rocks, but he swam back as quickly as he could into the next patch of still water. He clambered onto the rock and rested again.

He heard a shout from the beach but couldn't understand what they were saying. He supposed that they were asking if he was okay and waved to re-assure them that he was still alive and kicking.

Dan progressed along the remaining rocks as best he could until he was at the last one.

He looked out across the few hundred yards of seawater to the mainland on the other side. Not too far. In a swimming pool he would be able to swim that far in a few minutes and he'd sometimes swum that distance in the sea, but always on a bright sunny day when he was on holiday.

This was a different prospect. Even though Bez had said that this was low tide, the water was still moving fairly quickly. Dan presumed that it was the force of the wind that was creating the flow of the water.

He wouldn't be able to go directly across, he would need to swim in a diagonal direction to counter-act the current.

Dan felt the raining hitting the side of his face and looked up at the sky. It was getting very dark. The land on the opposite side was really just a silhouette now.

Don't hang around, he thought to himself and dived in. The cold of the water hit him once again and he tried to relax his breathing as he started a steady front crawl.

The waves weren't crashing over him out here in the open water, it was simply the rise and fall of a heavy swell. He tried to fix his aim on a particular point of land and every few strokes had a quick glance to reassure himself he wasn't off course.

Dan pushed gradually but strongly through the water, trying not to think about the darkness that was folding in around him or the depth of the sea beneath him.

After a little while, he glanced ahead, satisfied himself that he was still on course and risked a quick glance behind. Ramsey Island was a dark shape behind him and he guessed that he was halfway across.

He was pleased and tried not to think about how tired he was. The cold and the anxiety were leaching the strength away from him more quickly than he had expected.

Realised that he had increased his pace without thinking about it, he deliberately slowed his stroke rate again and tried to relax his breathing once more.

He gradually inched his way across the stretch of water until he looked up and realised with relief that he was nearing the headland in front of him. He looked at the land and remembered the coasteering day earlier in the week. It seemed like a million years ago now.

However the coastline was similar here: some low cliffs, in places there were huge strata of slate slanting into the water at 45 degrees, in other places boulders that had tumbled down from above. Dan headed for a jumble of boulders and allowed a wave to drive him forwards as they had done on the coasteering session. He raised his feet in front of him to cushion the impact as Ciaran had taught him and, as he made contact, managed to lean forwards and curl his fingers over the top of the rock to pull himself up.

He stood up, water surging around his legs and scrambled up a few boulders. The swim had exhausted him more than he had anticipated and he leant against a rock to get his breath back. Sitting there facing Ramsey Sound, he looked at the distance he had covered. It was almost completely dark now – but he could just make out the outline of the island. It seemed a long way off.

I've done it, he said to himself. Realising how cold he was, he decided to push on. He climbed up the rocks until he reached the footpath that ran along the top of the headland that overlooked the bottom end of the sound.

He half-walked and half-ran the mile to the lifeboat station and, as he crested the last rise and looked down on the building, he was relieved to see lights and people moving about.

Dan ran down the last part of the path and down the steps. A man was just coming out of the door as he approached and the man stopped in surprise at seeing Dan with just a t-shirt, his boxer shorts and his shoes.

"There are some people on Ramsey Island that need to be rescued," Dan blurted out.

"Pardon?" said the man. "What are you talking about? What people?"

"Do you know Geraint? He's one of the coxswains here."

"Geraint? Of course. My name's Dafydd, I'm one of the other coxswains. But I heard Geraint went out in the small lifeboat?"

"Well …" started Dan.

"Hang on," interrupted Dafydd. "You must be freezing. Let's get you inside and find you some clothes. And you can fill me in while we're getting the boat ready again."

They went inside but Dan insisted on explaining the situation before getting changed.

By the time he had finished, the crew had donned their overalls and the lifeboat was ready to go out again.

The boat slid down the slipway, splashed into the water and the engine roared as it quickly made for Ramsey Island.

Dafydd had stayed behind as another man had taken his turn to cox the lifeboat. "So you really swam across the sound in this weather?" he asked with a disbelieving look. "How long did it take you?"

"I've no idea," Dan shrugged. "It seemed to be a lifetime."

"Let's find you those clothes then," he said to Dan. "You must be freezing."

"Is Ciaran about?" asked Dan, as they climbed up to the control room. "I thought he was coming over to man the lifeboat station when we left?"

"He was here when we got back, but we let him go home again. He said he still wasn't feeling too good."

Dafydd found Dan some clothes and he got dressed as quickly as he could. He pulled on an old woollen jumper and at last felt some warmth start returning to his body.

Now that he had made sure the lifeboat was on its way, Dan's attention immediately turned to what he needed to do next.

"I'm going to head off now," he said to Dafydd who was looking out of the control room window across the sound.

Dafydd turned round, surprised. "You don't want to stay here and wait for your friends?"

"No, I need to go," Dan said. "Tell Bethan I said thanks for everything."

"Right …" Dafydd replied, confused.

Dan turned and headed down the control room steps. He grabbed the minibus car keys from the box by the overalls and ran out of the building.

He needed to get away as quickly as possible, before Andrew came back with the lifeboat. He wondered if he might have an hour or two head start because they would need to get Asha over the island on a stretcher.

Maybe I've just got time to nip back to Bethan's place to get my things, he wondered.

23. Curiosity Is The Father Of Regret. St Davids. Saturday Evening.

Dan pulled into the driveway of Alun House.

He slowed for a moment as he was surprised to see an old battered Peugot 205 parked just outside the front door. He decided to risk it and continued down the drive and around the back of the house.

He hoped the sound of the wind and rain had masked his passage across the gravel.

He didn't know who might be at the house, but he wanted to get his laptop, tent and other things and get away without being seen if possible. He would love to throw his bike in the back of the minibus as well if he could. After parking, he decided to load his bike first. He wheeled it out of the shed and lifted it into the back of the vehicle, trying to make as little noise as possible.

Dan slid as quietly as possible through the back door and slipped up the stairs. In his room, he quickly stuffed all his belongings into his rucksack.

He came back down the stairs, moving softly on the balls of his feet and taking each step slowly to keep any sound to a minimum.

As he reached the bottom of the stairs, he heard a frustrated voice from down the corridor say "stupid machine". He paused. It had sounded like Ciaran.

Dan listened and thought he heard the sound of fingers on a keyboard from the office. He looked along the corridor and saw light coming through the doorway. The electricity must be back on, he thought.

Curiosity got the better of him and he moved quietly along the hallway to peer through the crack in the doorway to the office.

It was Ciaran and the electricity was indeed back on. What was he doing here? Dan turned to leave and then stopped. He turned back to look at Ciaran again – he didn't look unwell. I'm going to regret this, he thought, but pushed open the door.

"How come you're here?" said Dan, stepping into the room. "I thought you were ill?"

"Jesus!" exclaimed Ciaran, jumping back from the computer as though it had electrocuted him. He looked up and a number of emotions flitted across his face: worry, surprise, relief, anxiety. "It's you Dan. What are you doing here?"

"I asked you first," smiled Dan. "I thought you were ill?"

"Er, I was just checking stuff for tomorrow."

"I don't think we'll have any trips tomorrow after what's happened today."

Ciaran nodded but didn't say anything. He didn't move and Dan saw another emotion in his expression: regret.

"Are you okay, Ciaran?" Dan asked. "Actually why aren't you asking how Bethan and the other people are?"

Ciaran sagged in the chair. "It wasn't my idea, Dan."

"What wasn't?"

Ciaran then glanced towards the window and Dan heard what had caught his attention. A large engined car was travelling quickly down the drive and then it drew to a stop, sliding on the gravel.

"They have a saying in Ireland," Ciaran said. "Touch the devil and you can't let go. That's happened to me."

"What are you talking about?" asked Dan and walked over to the window to look out.

He just caught a glimpse of someone coming to the front of the house, running through the rain. He heard the front door open with a bang and footsteps marching briskly down the hallway.

Dan turned and saw Rhys Jones walk through the doorway.

"Have you got it yet?" Rhys barked at Ciaran.

-o-o-o-

A few minutes earlier, Jess had been sitting in a café just up the road from Geddes Outdoor Sports.

She was sitting at a window table where she could see the entrance to Alun House and keep a look out for Cullen if he returned.

She had seen another person arrive fifteen minutes earlier, but then to her surprise and excitement saw Cullen drive past in the white Geddes minibus and turn into the driveway to the house.

What should I do now? she thought. She realised she couldn't restrain Cullen herself, but she didn't want to let him go again. If Cullen decided to drive off once more there would be nothing she could do about it without a car of her own. Jess decided to run to the small police station to see if PC Evans was back.

She left money for her tea and set off up the road. She was pleased to see the white police Range Rover was back again and the station door was open.

She ran in and PC Evans looked up on hearing her rush through the doorway.

"Can you arrest our man now?" she blurted out, not quite sure how to say it. However the young policeman was already standing up.

"I was wondering if you would come back," PC Evans said, putting on his helmet and his coat. "Where is he?"

"He's just come back to Geddes Outdoor Sports."

"Okay, let's go," he said. "And you can tell me more about this man on the way."

They walked briskly up to Alun House and Jess explained what Cullen had done. At the top of the drive they stopped to look at the house. There was a Peugot 205 parked by the front door and a light was on in the office. Before entering the property, PC Evans called his colleague for backup.

As they walked down the driveway, they saw a light go on in an upstairs room. It was now mid-evening and the house was otherwise in darkness apart from the light in the office downstairs.

"I just want to confirm where your man is and then we'll wait for my colleague," said the policeman. "He only lives ten minutes away so he shouldn't be long. First, let's check that the minibus you saw him arrive in is parked round the back. They normally park them there."

They left the drive and skirted round the bushes to the back of the house. The white minibus was still parked there.

"The back door is open, PC Evans," Jess whispered.

"You can call me Tom," he said and moved quietly towards the doorway and looked in.

The hallway was in darkness and he slipped in silently. Jess followed him.

They moved noiselessly along the corridor in the direction of the light at the front of the house. Just as they passed the stairway, they heard a light switch upstairs and very quiet footsteps on the floor above. Tom and Jess slipped into the darkened room opposite the office and discovered that they were in the kitchen.

They listened to the person coming slowly down the stairs, moving along the corridor and saw him looking through the office doorway.

Jess saw that it was Cullen and almost shouted, but held herself back. Tom glanced at her with raised eyebrows as if to say: is that your man? Jess nodded emphatically.

After a couple of seconds, they saw Cullen go into the office and heard him start talking to the person who was in there.

Then they heard a car coming down the driveway.

"That should be my colleague now," Tom whispered and then paused. "Mind you, I didn't think he'd just come noisily down the drive."

The car outside skidded to a halt on the gravel and they heard the scrunch of footsteps followed by the front door banging open.

Tom was surprised to see local businessman, Rhys Jones, march past the kitchen doorway and into the office.

"Have you got it yet?" he heard him bark.

-o-o-o-

Ciaran's head drooped in submission.

"Well?" growled Jones again, wondering why Ciaran hadn't answered his question. Was the boy stupid?

Ciaran glanced at Dan and Jones followed his gaze, for the first time noticing Dan standing by the window. Surprise flitted across his face and then annoyance. "What are you doing here?" he shouted.

"I was thinking of asking you the same question," Dan replied. He turned to Ciaran. "What's he doing here, Ciaran?"

"I'm sorry, Dan. Like I said, I've touched the devil." Ciaran paused for a moment and then blurted out: "I was really short of money, still owed all my university fees, overdraft, credit cards and I met Rhys in the pub one night and he asked me to print out all of Bethan's bookings for the last year in exchange for a thousand quid."

"Shut up, Colin," Jones ordered.

"It's Ciaran, you idiot!" Ciaran shouted at him. "I've had enough of your crap now." He then turned back to Dan. "I told him where to go, but then I had the bank chasing me to clear my overdraft and a few days later I saw him again. He offered me five thousand pounds in cash and I stupidly said yes. He gave me half the money up front and then never paid me the other half."

"Shut up, you fool," said Jones. "You'll get yourself into trouble as well, you know."

Ciaran ignored him. "Anyway I was stupid. I should have known it wouldn't just be a one-off thing. He then blackmailed me. Told me that he'd tell Bethan I'd given him the information for nothing and that she'd sack me. And he made me give him more and more information, always with a couple of hundred quid each time but never enough that I could pay off my bills or anything."

"What about the cutting of the tyres and the climbing rope?" asked Dan. "And the boat today? You're not sick, are you? You sabotaged the boat and then pretended you were ill."

"No, I didn't do any of those things," Ciaran insisted. "It was all Rhys. And he told me last night that I wasn't to go to work today, because he wanted me to do something for him. He made me," Ciaran finished pathetically.

"That's nonsense," Jones cried.

"Why did he do all this?" Dan asked Ciaran. "I know he owes a lot of money to the banks, but how would buying another house help that?"

"You keep out of my personal affairs," Jones said pointedly.

"And he owns the two properties next door," said Dan.

Jones looked at him. "How do you know that?" he exclaimed in surprise.

"I heard him talking to Hugh Gardiner one time …" said Ciaran.

"That guy we saw in the pub a couple of nights ago?"

"Yes. He's on the city council, and he's also on the planning committee. They were talking about some big new property development they were going to build on this site. Hugh was in on it as well."

"You think you know everything," Jones said. "Well you don't. There is nothing wrong with these development plans. A large client has asked me to put together a portfolio of land so that they can build a holiday village here – a series of nice holiday units with indoor and outdoor swimming pools, tennis courts, the lot. And Hugh is on board because he understood how much it will benefit the town with increased tourism revenues."

"And how much benefit will you get from it, Jones?" asked Dan.

"That's none of your business."

"It is my business if you put people's lives in danger."

"Ha," said Jones. "You can't prove anything."

"They can if I tell them everything that you told me," said Ciaran quietly. "I'll tell them how you boasted to me after each incident."

"Shut up, you fool. You're as complicit as me if you do that."

"That's fine. I deserve to go to prison. You've put people's lives in danger, Rhys, and I should have stopped you, but I was too weak. They're my friends as well." Ciaran shook his head despondently.

At that moment, they heard the sound of another car travelling down the gravel driveway.

Dan was still by the window and glanced out. Jones saw the surprise on Dan's face and moved over to look for himself.

"It's the police," Jones said. He looked at Ciaran accusingly. "You called them."

Ciaran was just about to argue, but just shrugged. "It doesn't matter who called them. It's what I wanted anyway."

"Well I'm not hanging around," Jones said and started walking towards the door.

PC Evans chose that moment to step into the room. Jones took a step backwards.

"Tom Evans," Jones said. "Where did you spring from?"

"I was just next door in the kitchen," said the policeman. "Listening to this interesting conversation."

"Don't forget, your mother works for me," said Jones.

"And she's hated every minute of it."

There was a moment where nobody said anything and nobody moved. Dan supposed afterwards that Jones must have been thinking back through everything that he'd said in the conversation. And he must have decided that he had incriminated himself, because the next moment he pushed Tom Evans in the chest and bolted through the doorway.

Jess was in the hall and tried to grab him, but he pushed her away too.

Jones ran out of the front door. Tom recovered his balance and started chasing after him. He shouted out of the front door to his colleague: "Max, grab him. Rhys Jones. Grab him."

PC Max Morgan was just getting out of his car and was surprised to see the owner of the local estate agents come running out of Bethan Geddes' house. He thought he heard his friend Tom shout something about grabbing him, but surely he couldn't have said that he should grab Rhys Jones. He was here to help with the arrest of some fugitive who used to work for a bank in London.

He stood by his car as Rhys Jones ran past him and jumped into his BMW. Max had never liked that car. Well he liked it really, but he didn't like Rhys Jones and the fact that he owned it.

"Max, you blithering idiot, stop him," shouted Tom Evans as he came charging out of the front door. "Rhys Jones. Stop him."

Max might not have been sure the first time, but he wasn't going to argue with Tom a second time. Tom seemed quite certain that Rhys was the person he wanted. As Jones started his BMW,

Max jumped back through the open door of his police car, slipped it quickly into gear and drove across the back of Jones' BMW X5.

The large four-wheel drive car reversed into the side of the police car with a crunch, but it stopped Jones in his tracks. He slammed the BMW X5 into first gear and tried to move forwards but he was too close to the house and the delay provided Tom Evans with enough time to get to the car, rip the driver's door open and pull out the ignition key.

-o-o-o-

Dan had watched Jones push his way out of the office and saw the policeman chase him out of the building. Ciaran stood up and looked out of the window at the commotion and Dan took the opportunity to step quietly out of the office and into the hall. He glanced to his left and saw a woman standing in the front doorway, also looking at what was happening out on the drive. He thought that she looked like the woman who had come to the office earlier in the day to ask about a kayaking trip. What was she doing here?

Dan picked up his rucksack which he'd left at the bottom of the stairs and walked swiftly to the back door.

Still raining, he thought as he exited the house. He threw his rucksack through the door of the minibus and started the engine.

-o-o-o-

Jess was standing in the doorway at the front of the house watching PC Tom Evans reach into Rhys Jones' car and take the ignition keys. She saw PC Morgan's face as he walked round his car and saw the front wing hanging off and the wheel leaning in on itself.

"Look at the car, Tom," said PC Morgan. "Terry isn't going to be happy."

At least they had stopped Jones getting away, she thought.

Where's Cullen? she thought suddenly and then she saw the white minibus come speeding round from the side of the house. For a brief moment the remaining headlight on PC Morgan's car illuminated Cullen's face at the steering wheel.

The driveway was blocked by Jones' BMW and the crumpled police car but Cullen drove up onto the grass, around the cars and back onto the driveway.

He accelerated up to the gate and turned out onto the open road.

Jess stood there motionless, just watching.

I don't care about Terry, she thought to herself, whoever he is. Andrew's not going to be happy. Not happy at all.

24. It Never Rains But It Pours. Haverfordwest. Sunday.

"So you let him get away again?" Richard said.

"Me?" said Andrew, in an exasperated voice.

It was the next day and Andrew was standing in the train station at Haverfordwest talking to his boss on the phone. It was still raining heavily.

"I'm only joking, Andrew," his boss said.

"It was your Jessica who lost him," Andrew pointed out.

"*My* Jessica? I don't have a Jessica," smiled Richard. "Anyway bring me up to date."

"Cullen drove away in the minibus last night and the local police spent thirty minutes sorting out this Rhys Jones character before they were able to get a car in pursuit. At least Jessica got them to do that. They seemed far more interested in Jones and some guy called Ciaran MacGwyverdine who had been helping him."

"I heard they found the minibus last night," said Richard.

"Aye, a couple of hours later. Cullen had driven it off a road on the way to Fishguard and it was on fire. The local police were just sitting there waiting for the fire brigade to come and put it out. But by then I'd got off the island and drove over to where the minibus was. I couldn't believe that it had caught fire in that pouring rain with him inside. Too convenient. So I got them to start asking around."

"And?"

"Nobody had seen anything in the nearby village so I got them to widen the search. I had them banging on doors through the night. At eight o'clock this morning they found a resident in a neighbouring village who had noticed somebody cycling along the road to Haverfordwest yesterday evening. He remembered it because it was raining so hard and it was so late at night. And the guy didn't have any lights."

"No lights? Must have been difficult cycling on country roads in the dark," mused Richard.

"Cullen didn't want to be seen, but fortunately this local resident had been out walking his dog before going to bed and Cullen went right past him. Gave him a hell of a shock apparently. Anyway, I didn't think that he might have had a bike in the back of the minibus. He obviously dumped the minibus on the Fishguard road to make us look in that direction, but then set off to Haverfordwest on his bike. It gave him just enough time because by the time we twigged he was already on the first train out."

"So somebody at the station remembers him? He was definitely there?"

"Aye, he cycled in at six o'clock, paid by cash and left his bike here. The description fits as well. I got here to the station at nine o'clock by which time he could have been somewhere like Bristol and then anywhere in the rail network. I've got the local guys phoning the train staff and also the staff at the main intersections where he could have changed, but it's pointless. Nobody will remember him and he could be anywhere in the country by this evening."

"Oh well," said Richard. "At least you got this other guy."

"Jones?" Andrew snorted. "I don't care about him."

"What about your desire for truth and justice? This person endangered the lives of dozens of people. Why did he do it? Presumably he would have benefited financially somehow from the purchase of this house?"

"Aye," nodded Andrew. "He had been appointed by a group wanting to buy a plot of land large enough to build a holiday village and the place owned by Bethan Geddes was the last one he needed. Once Jones had put the package of property together he was going to sell it on to this group for a profit of two million pounds."

"And they've got enough to convict him I hope?"

"I believe so. This Ciaran person is going to testify against him in exchange for a lesser sentence and Jessica recorded the whole conversation on her phone."

"So there you go," said Richard. "You got one bad guy."

"So why do I feel like I've lost?" Andrew said.

"Hang on a sec," said Richard. "Nigel's just come into the office."

Andrew faintly heard Nigel's voice: "You're not going to believe this. He's still doing it."

"Who's still doing what?" said Richard.

"Put him on speaker," Andrew said loudly.

"Hang on," said Richard. "Okay you're on speaker, Andrew. Who's still doing what, Nigel?"

"Cullen ..." he started and then paused, unsure how to continue.

"Spit it out man," said Richard. "What's he doing?"

"He's still taking money."

"What?" said Richard. "When?"

"Over the last few months. There was even a transfer yesterday at six o'clock in the morning."

"Yesterday! How do you know this?" asked Richard.

"The ZBS audit team just called me and they're a bit worried I think. He's taken a lot of money this time."

"What, more than £10million?"

"Yes, a lot more."

"Well, how much more?"

"They haven't worked it all out yet."

"How do they know it was him?"

"Actually they don't know for sure. But they're hoping it's him."

"Why?"

"Because if it's not Cullen, then they've got somebody else stealing money."

Richard sighed. "How did he get into their systems?" he asked.

"They haven't worked that out yet either," replied Nigel. "They're working on the assumption that he set up access for himself when he worked there."

There was a pause as they all processed the news.

Eventually Richard spoke. "Did you hear all that, Andrew?"

"Aye," Andrew replied. "I'm not actually that surprised."

"Really?" said Richard. "Why not?"

"He said something to me when we were on the island about having started something that needed finishing. I don't know, it just sounded like a work in progress." Andrew paused for a moment. "And now that I think about it, at one of the places where he worked, the guy said that Cullen was often on his laptop for long periods. I remember thinking at the time that it was strange – I wondered why he needed a laptop at all. But now we know why."

"What are we going to do?" asked Richard.

"Well the blithering idiots in their IT department need to make sure he can't log in any more,"Andrew said. Other than that, nothing's changed. We simply monitor his friends and family, keep an eye on his credit cards, all the usual things."

"So we just have to wait for him to pop up somewhere again or make another mistake?" Richard said. "That could be months or years."

"He's starting to get tired of running, Richard," Andrew said. "We're going to get him at some point. If you never give up, you can never lose. And you know me, I never give up."

The End

See below for details of the next book in the series.

-o-o-o-

Author's Note

All the people in this book are fictional, but all the places are real. Pembrokeshire is a beautiful part of the country and you really can go white water kayaking in Ramsey Sound. The rocks that stretch out into the sound are really called The Bitches as many boats have run aground on them over the years.

Geddes Outdoor Sports is fictional but in St Davids there are many businesses running kayaking and climbing days. They invented coasteering in St Davids and I encourage you to try it –

it's beautiful and relaxing at times and at other times it's thrilling and scary – you'll never forget jumping off a fifty foot cliff into a pool of seawater.

I have worked on a business system for a company that really does surveillance on behalf of insurance companies – so if you're claiming for whiplash then don't go and play football - somebody might be watching!

Ramsey Island (*Ynys Dewi*) is owned and managed by the RSPB and well worth a visit. The island has spectacular bird cliffs, coastal scenery and heathland. Ramsey Sound has the most important Grey Seal breeding colony in southern Britain, with over 400 seal pups born each autumn. It is one of the best sites in Wales to see Choughs and other breeding species include Ravens, Common Buzzards, Peregrines, Northern Wheatears, gulls, auks, Manx Shearwaters, Razorbills and Guillemots.

Contrary to what I said in the story, Ramsey Island actually has a permanent population of two human residents (the RSPB warden and his wife who live in a farmhouse there), but I chose to gloss over that particular fact. Poetic license, you could say. You can visit the island during the summer: tourist boats sail to and around the island, seven days a week from Easter to October. You can catch them from Saint Justinian's RNLI lifeboat station on the mainland.

The lifeboat station itself is open to visitors and you can see the impressive setup they have there – despite the remoteness of the location, the self-righting fast-slipway lifeboat, RNLB Garside, is packed full of the latest technology which improves the safety of the crew and also enables them to save more lives. When built the Garside cost approximately £530,000 but underwent a refit in 1999 at a cost of almost £100,000. For further information go to www.rnli.org.uk/stdavids or their own website: http://stdavids-rnli.org.uk

And, by the way, I have a friend who really did flip his radiator off with a ski-walker. You probably thought that story sounded a bit far-fetched.

Rod Gordon
rod@rrgordon.com

P.S. By the way, if you liked this book then you may like to add a short review comment to Amazon – it would be much appreciated. Just go to the Amazon site, find the book and click on the "write a customer review" button near the bottom of the page. Many thanks!

-o-o-o-

We hope you enjoyed this book.
*The third book in the series is entitled **Rydal Water**.*

Dan has been on the run for nearly three years and he's tired. He's tired of the relentless need to keep moving and constantly looking over his shoulder - and he's only been able to snatch a few minutes with the woman he loves in the last 18 months. Andrew Muir is the investigator assigned to bring Dan to justice – and he knows that Muir never gives up.

With the help of an old friend Dan makes plans to resolve matters, once and for all, but he doesn't realise the destruction this will cause until it's nearly too late.

Rydal Water is a fast-moving thriller which contrasts the splendid isolation of the two main characters in a snowbound village in the Lake District with a plot which has a frighteningly believable impact on the economic infrastructure of the entire world.

To purchase Rydal Water – or to read a sample chapter – then please go to Amazon and search for "rr gordon rydal water" or go to http://www.amazon.co.uk/dp/B00AUICYNI

To find out about other books by RR Gordon please visit www.rrgordon.com.

To subscribe to the newsletter and receive notification when future books are published simply email subscribe@rrgordon.com with 'Subscribe' in the Subject box.

-o-o-o-

*You may also wish to read **Leap** by RR Gordon:*

Just after finishing his engineering degree, Ben Smith meets his dream girl - and is offered his dream job: working on the next generation of engines to be used in the first manned expedition to another planet.

However his career is over before it's begun as he uncovers a conspiracy in his new company, involving those closest to him. For Ben the space mission was to have been an opportunity to reach to the edge of our solar system, but others see a chance for personal gain.

Set against the backdrop of exploration, Leap is a classic thriller, which tells the tale of a young man's desire to fight for his beliefs and his need to win the girl that he loves.

Praise for Leap:

"Fantastic book, with plenty of twists and turns and a shocking ending."
"A very enjoyable book, written by a natural storyteller."

To purchase Leap – or to read a sample chapter – then please go to Amazon and search for "rr gordon leap" or go to http://www.amazon.co.uk/dp/B005F6EBX6

Printed in Great Britain
by Amazon

59404594R00119